Other Books by this Author:

Out of the Storm

The Bridge Series

Deception Bridge

BROKEN
Contracts

♣♥ GLORIA BOSTIC ♠♦

Year of the Book
135 Glen Avenue
Glen Rock, PA 17327

ISBN 13: 978-1-945670-69-5

ISBN 10: 1-945670-69-X

Library of Congress Control Number: 2017918201

DEDICATION

To all the mothers and fathers, sisters and brothers, sons and daughters, friends and loved ones of those struggling with addiction.

And...

To every person who rises each morning and makes the choice not to have that drink or use any other drug that once held power over them. By accepting that there is a Power greater than yourself, you have become empowered. You are my heroes.

Acknowledgments

I'd like to thank all those who helped me understand and write about a subject that touches so many of our lives.

Thanks to those who shared their knowledge of the justice system and those who shared their knowledge of addiction and recovery. I truly appreciate your help.

As always, I also am thankful to my family and friends, my critique group and fellow authors, and my publisher for their encouragement and patience as I follow my dreams.

CHAPTER ONE

Valerie Reed's jaw dropped, along with some of the cards she'd been shuffling, as Kathy's revelation ripped open the old wound.

"Yeah, I saw her this afternoon when I stopped at the grocery store on the way home. She looked awful." Kathy James was the newest member of their bridge group and a bit of a gossip, but she meant no harm.

The first time she'd joined them, Val had been alarmed by the tiny diamond sparkling on the side of her nose and the writing tattooed on her inner forearm. But it hadn't taken long to find out her instincts were wrong. The young woman was endearing, and gossiping was simply her way of reaching out to people.

Today Kathy was sharing news about a former card club member, Susan Walters. "She had her little girl with her, Lizzie, such a cutie-pie with that curly red hair. Oh, and then Susan snapped at me, 'Her name is Elizabeth!'" Kathy rolled her eyes. "I'd forgotten the only one who can get away with calling her Lizzie is her daddy."

Val and her best friend, Bonnie Dixon, exchanged wary glances.

"But, like I said, Susan looked just awful."

"What do you mean?" Bonnie asked.

"Well, I'm not saying this to be cruel, but she's gotten too skinny. Her cheeks are all sunken in—like she's anorexic—and honestly," Kathy paused, then went on in a hushed voice, "She's aged."

Val sat in stunned silence. When she thought of the woman who had nearly destroyed her marriage, she remembered a curvy, petite blonde with porcelain skin.

"Do you think maybe she's been sick?" Sarah asked.

"Maybe…" Kathy hedged, "or maybe it's something else. You know she and Marty split up about six months ago."

Val dropped the cards mid-shuffle. "Are… are you sure?" she stammered, hastily scooping them up, trying to cover her shock and dismay.

"Yeah. It's a real shame… and her with the little one. From what I understand, she and Marty had a big fight one day, and he stormed out."

Bonnie broke the stunned silence. "Well, that is a shame, but we'd better get back on track if we're going to finish this rubber before midnight."

Everyone laughed, so Val shakily dealt the cards. When she arranged her hand, she was relieved to see so few face cards and no strong suit. The news about Susan had her head spinning. "Dealer passes," Val said.

"One heart," was Sarah's response.

Bonnie studied her cards and finally said, "Two clubs." Val looked across the table at her partner and rolled her eyes.

Kathy couldn't help laughing at the unspoken communication. "Watch it, you two," she joked before jumping to three hearts.

After Val passed again, Sarah took a breath and declared three no trump.

Passes round the table gave Sarah the contract and her smile broadened when her partner, Kathy, turned over cards which complemented her own.

During Sarah's five years in the bridge group, she had learned a lot from playing every Thursday evening. As one of Bonnie's grad students she'd seemed so nervous at first, not knowing anyone and unsure of herself. When Sarah started dating Val's son, Craig, it was cause for celebration. Now, five years later, as a practicing psychologist, her confidence showed as she even managed to finesse two over-tricks.

"Way to go, partner!" Kathy had managed to sit quietly while she was dummy, but it hadn't been easy. "So, Sarah, have you seen her lately around the hospital?"

"What? Oh, Susan you mean?" Sarah looked heavenward. "Hmm, I guess it's been at least a year. I think she's still at Madison General, but she doesn't work in the Psych Unit." Putting her finger on her chin she shook her head. "Yeah, I can't remember exactly, but it might be longer."

Kathy looked from her to Val and Bonnie, but both women shook their heads. "Oh, well take my word for it. She's changed. Maybe you're right, Sarah, and she's sick. Either that or the split is really taking a toll."

Val registered the look of concern on her daughter-in-law's face, but her own mind went somewhere else. Was it only six years ago she'd nearly lost everything? She remembered the sleepless nights and the headaches… the terrible headaches.

But that was then and this is now.

"Well, it looks like Sarah and Kathy are the big winners tonight." Bonnie's voice called her back to the present. "Val, would you help me carry these things to the kitchen for Kathy?"

"I can help," Sarah chimed in, but Bonnie put up a hand.

"No need. We've got this, right, Val?"

Val grabbed a couple of the snacks and headed for the other room. She put the glass dishes on the counter and turned to find Bonnie waiting expectantly.

"Are you okay, child? You look like you might have one of those headaches like you used to get."

Val's stomach lurched, and she felt her cheeks flush. "Yeah, well she definitely took me by surprise. We'll talk later, okay?" The final word was hardly out of her mouth before Kathy barged into the kitchen, and they both fell silent.

"Thanks, ladies! Hey, what's going on?" Kathy laughed nervously, her insecurities showing. "You weren't talking about me, were you?"

"Not a chance!" Bonnie gave her young friend a hug. "You know we love you," she added with a wink. And they did. Even though she tended to be a bit of a gossip, her innocence was endearing. She had added a new energy to their group when she joined them the year before, and her excitement and enthusiasm were contagious.

"Well, it's getting late, girls." Sarah poked her head in and asked, "Are we heading home or is there a party going on in here?"

Not in the mood for a party, Valerie Reed wanted nothing more than to be alone.

♥

On the walk out to the car Val breathed in the cool night air. She was still too preoccupied to be aware of the usual landmarks on the drive home. She didn't even notice the shiny red sportscar right on her bumper. And she almost didn't see the stop sign at the busy intersection of Diamond Avenue and Starlight Drive. The blast of a horn made her slam on the brakes before sliding into the intersection.

Lord, help me... Focus, Val! She gripped the wheel a little tighter, looked to be sure it was safe, then eased through the intersection.

The driver behind her leaned on his horn and followed right on her tail. *Damn!* Val glared at him in the rearview mirror. She wanted nothing more than to be home. She took a deep, calming breath and finally turned onto her street, relieved to see light shining through the living-room curtains.

Once inside, Val hung her keys on the hook by the door and leaned on the kitchen counter.

"Hi, sweetheart. I'm in the study," called her husband. She knew Andy was working on his paper again tonight. He wanted to submit it for publication by week's end.

He didn't always go to their son Craig's on bridge night the way he used to, and Val had to admit she enjoyed knowing he was home waiting for her. But tonight, she paused before joining him in the study.

"I'll be there in a minute," she called as she grabbed a bottle of water from the fridge. She grappled with whether or not to mention Kathy's bit of gossip. They didn't have secrets anymore—not since they'd healed their marriage. But this was sure to stir up issues. Would it open old wounds? And was it worth bringing up at all? After all, it was only gossip.

Val headed for the study, bottle of water in her hand and a smile on her face. She leaned down and planted a kiss on her husband's cheek, brushed her hand over his close-cropped hair, and asked, "Are you almost ready to turn in?"

Andy tossed her a kiss and nodded, already giving his attention back to the task before him.

Val glanced back over her shoulder, then headed for the bedroom… and the Tylenol. *No sense bothering him with this right now. It can wait.*

CHAPTER TWO

"**H**urry up, Julie! Are you going to be in there all night?" It was Sarah's youngest son, Bobby, that she heard as soon as she opened the front door. Seconds later he followed with, "Well, it's about time."

"Yeah, whatever," was Julie's only response before going into her own room and closing the door harder than necessary.

Sarah was in no way alarmed by what had become a nightly bedtime ritual. Sometimes she thought her youngest son purposely delayed his bedtime prep so he could give his big sister a hard time.

"Hi Mom, you're home early, aren't you?" Sarah's stepdaughter, Mia, greeted her as she headed toward her own bedroom.

Sarah glanced at the time on her Fitbit. "Yeah, it didn't take Kathy and I long to clobber your Grandma and Aunt Bonnie tonight," she winked.

Bonnie Dixon wasn't really the kids' aunt, but she was like a member of the family, so the children had always addressed her that way.

Mia's eyes widened in fake horror, "Oh, I'm gonna tell Grandma what you said!" before she gave Sarah a quick kiss on the cheek and dashed off to bed.

"Don't you dare!" Sarah called after her with a chuckle. She was grateful to have such an easy, loving relationship with her stepchildren. When she'd first met Mia and her younger brother, Cody, they'd recently lost their mother in a tragic accident, and when her friendship with their father, Craig, developed into more than friendship, she had wondered if they could ever accept her as part of the family.

She needn't have worried.

By the time she and Craig walked down the aisle, the children had already come to love her. They knew it was okay to talk about Jenny—the mother they'd lost that dreadful night—and that Sarah honored her memory just as she honored the memory of her late husband who'd lost his battle with cancer several years earlier.

But Sarah wasn't thinking about past losses when she plopped down on the sofa next to Craig. "Guess who made three notrump with two over-tricks tonight?'

"I think that big grin on your face is a clue," he laughed. "That's my girl. You'll soon be ready for tournament play."

She sat up and looked at her husband with righteous indignation. "You mean you don't think I'm ready now?" But she couldn't maintain that façade for long before she too was laughing. "No, I don't think I'm quite there yet. I'll stick with playing socially, thank you." She snuggled in and nearly purred as Craig wrapped his arm around her shoulders and kissed the top of her head.

"So what news did Little Miss Kathy have to share this week?"

Sarah could almost hear Craig grinning as he asked. He seemed to find her bridge partner's newscasts quite entertaining. "Well, actually she did share something interesting—and a little concerning—about Susan Walters. You remember her, right?"

"Uh-huh. Yeah, she used to go to our church."

"Yeah, that's her. Well, Kathy ran into her and says she and her husband split. They have a little girl. Such a shame. And Kathy said she looks bad."

"Yeah. That's rough." Craig pulled her closer. "Not everyone has what we do." With his free hand he lifted her chin and kissed her tenderly.

Sarah felt a familiar tingle go through her body and moved in closer. Though she was inclined to do more, she gently pulled back. "Hmm, I think I'd better go say goodnight to the kids before you make me forget."

"To be continued…" he said wistfully.

She glanced back, "Definitely," she added in her most seductive voice.

"Grrrr…"

♥

When Sarah and Craig entered their master suite and closed the door behind them forty-five minutes later, all four children were finally settled and fast asleep. As much as they both loved the kids, they cherished their quiet time together, to unwind and reconnect at the end of each of their busy days.

Craig didn't take long to get ready for bed and was sitting, hands behind his head, leaning against the pillows while Sarah finished removing her makeup and brushing out her hair. "I thought for sure that freshman was going to fall asleep in class today," he said about one of his American History students. "I kept waiting for his chin to fall off his fist," he snickered.

Craig taught at Madison University, and as much as he loved history and was known to make it come alive, she knew it could be a real challenge with some of the sleep-deprived kids in his morning classes.

This is when Sarah might have told her husband about being ready to discharge a client she was doing grief counseling with. She loved her career as a psychotherapist working in the same agency as Craig's dad, but tonight she had something else on her mind.

"I've been thinking. It's been a long time since our surprise pregnancy and, you know, losing the baby, and well, we've talked about how we have room for one more in our family." She'd been sitting on the side of the bed with her back to her husband. She turned slowly and added, "And I was thinking maybe if you're serious—I mean if you really think we should—well maybe it's time to…" She saw her husband's face transform into happy anticipation. She hurried on, "I mean, I'm not getting any younger."

She didn't get a chance to say any more as Craig slid down onto the pillows and pulled her down with him. His eyes gave her his answer even before he spoke the words. "Let's make a baby."

Chapter Three

Val tossed and turned with weird, disturbing dreams waking her every hour. Morning brought a new resolve to talk to Andy about what she'd heard the night before. She set his big mug of coffee on the island as he rushed into the kitchen.

"Ah, thank you, sweetheart. I really need that this morning. Oh, and no time for breakfast now. I have a nine o'clock client—second visit—and I've gotta review my notes on his case before he comes in." Val saw the wrinkle between his brows deepen. "PTSD. I'm afraid this is gonna be a rough one."

"A veteran?"

"No, actually severe abuse from childhood reared its ugly head. Could be a long road back." Andy drained his cup and glanced at his watch. "Gotta go. See ya around four o'clock?"

"Sure thing. I should be here." Val tilted her head back to accept his kiss as he headed for the garage. "Love you."

Andy turned back, embraced his wife and indulged in a much more thorough goodbye. "And I love you," he said when their lips parted.

Val read the sincerity of his words in his eyes. His affair with Susan Walters, though brief, had been crushing. She was sure it was only through God's grace, her husband had truly repented. And through His grace, she had learned to trust Andy again. Their love and commitment to each other had grown even stronger in the years that followed.

The further shock of discovering Susan was pregnant—and fearing the baby might be Andy's—was relieved when they saw the baby's red hair. Little chance that could have come from Andy's brown-haired genes. They were convinced the trait had to come from Susan's red-headed husband, Marty. That is, until they'd attended Andy's uncle's funeral and spotted a little boy with strawberry blond hair.

And after much prayer, they had decided to leave it alone. Susan and Marty would be good parents, and after all, Elizabeth was probably Marty's little girl.

Now Val sat stirring her second cup of coffee and wondering if she should be stirring up anything else. She carried the mug into her home office and tried to push the nagging doubt out of her mind. Freelance writing was a luxury requiring self-discipline—not usually a problem for Val—and allowed her the freedom to help out with the grandkids when needed. Now that they were all in school, she wasn't needed as much, but she liked knowing she could help out when one of the four kids got sick.

What's going on with you, Susan? The thought jumped out at Val in the middle of reading over the article she was trying to edit. She realized she had no idea what she'd just read. *And what happened to your marriage?* Val stared out the window. Unable to focus, she got up and wandered across the room to stand beside it.

It was one of those early autumn days allowing a brief revisit of summer warmth. Multi-colored leaves lingered on the trees and lay on the ground beneath them. Val spun and grabbed the sweater off the back of her chair. The article could wait.

She breathed in the crisp air, exhaled tension, and headed down the path from the back deck to the edge of their property. She crossed onto the gravel walkway that led down toward the creek. Once under the trees, she slipped into her sweater. It was cooler here where the sun didn't reach, but she loved this spot.

Her favorite big flat rock beckoned, and she heeded its call. The sun was at the perfect angle to warm her and her rock-seat. It wasn't long before she pulled her arms out of the sweater. The stream bubbled over the rocks and glistened in the sun. Val found the peace she was looking for—and knew she'd find—in her special spot. "Thank you, Lord," she whispered. A hawk soared above.

"Playing tag, guys?" She laughed as two squirrels scampered across the ground darting up and down one tree after another. She listened to a couple of birds calling back and forth from somewhere high above. *Oh, I'm going to miss this.* Val dreaded the coming of winter and her self-imposed imprisonment indoors. The cold bothered her more as she got older, and she wondered how she'd stand it when she actually got old.

Val wasn't sure how much time had passed before she remembered her deadline and dragged herself back to the house. She didn't allow the cell phone in her peaceful spot, so she picked it up and saw the missed call.

"Hey, Bonnie. Sorry I missed you. I was out on my rock." She had shared the spot with her best friend years ago where they'd sat side by side sipping tea, soaking in sunshine, talking, and then praying together when her marriage to Andy had been threatened.

"Are you okay, Val?" Bonnie's concern was obvious.

"Yeah, I am. Hearing about Susan last night, well, it was like an ugly ghost from the past jumped out at me." She sighed. "But the point is, that's the past, and I think it will be best left there… So, that's where I'm going to leave it."

When the call ended a few minutes later, Val assured herself Susan, Marty, and *their child* were not her concern. She dismissed all thoughts of them and became lost in her work.

Forty minutes later Val hit 'send' and submitted her article. She put the leftover meatloaf from the previous night's dinner in the microwave for lunch, but was interrupted when her cell phone rang again. *Now what?* She thought it might be Buddy from the paper telling her the article wouldn't work. Grabbing the phone, she let out her breath when she saw Sarah's picture on the caller ID.

"Good morning, Sarah… No, you're not interrupting at all. What's up?"

She had grown to love her daughter-in-law in much the same way as she had cherished her son's first wife, Jenny. No one could ever take Jenny's place, but Sarah had certainly helped Craig heal after Jenny's death. Val would have treasured her for that alone even if she hadn't been such an endearing young woman.

"I hate to ask, but I got a call from the school. It's Mia. She was fine this morning. At least she didn't say anything about not feeling well, but the nurse said she's complaining of a sore throat, and she has a fever."

"Say no more, Sarah. I've got this." Val smiled into the phone. Being a work-from-home grandma had its perks.

♥

Mia loved school and rarely ever missed a day so Val knew the child hoped her sore throat wouldn't make her stay home.

"Grandma," she groaned, "Mom's gonna think it's strep again and make me go to the doctor's."

"I understand, sweetie, but I've got to agree with her." Val put the thermometer under her granddaughter's tongue. "We just love and worry about you."

Mia frowned, and Val understood.

The thermometer beeped and read 103.4. "Yep, looks like you're going to have to see Dr. Lynch again."

"Aw, Grandma, you know what he's gonna say," Mia pulled the blanket up under her chin and rolled over to face the window.

Val sat on the side of the bed and stroked her hair. She didn't like the idea of surgery for her granddaughter either, but the doctor had warned it might be the only answer.

"I know, sweetie. It's kind of scary, but I promise, if you get those tonsils out, it won't be so bad. You won't get sick and have to miss so much school."

No answer.

"Here, let's get that fever down."

She gave Mia Tylenol and rubbed her back until she heard the girl's breathing slow. Once Mia fell asleep, Val tiptoed out of the room, pulled the phone from her pocket, and called her daughter-in-law.

"Hi, Sarah. We're at the house, and she's asleep. Her fever is up to 103.4 now." Val offered to call Dr. Lynch and schedule an appointment, then added, "My guess is we'll soon be scheduling a visit to the hospital."

Chapter Four

Susan Walters stared at the blank TV screen. She swirled the amber liquid in her tumbler, loving the sound of the ice cubes clinking against the sides of the glass. Raising it to her lips, she took a drink and enjoyed the sensation of warmth all the way down.

The harsh ring of the phone snapped her back to reality, and she glanced at the time. *Oh jeez!* It was almost time to meet the school bus on the corner. Even though Susan was sure Elizabeth could make it to their front door by herself—she was almost six years old, after all—she knew that would be unacceptable. With horror she imagined the bus driver's reaction if she wasn't there to meet her child.

Susan stood up, took a moment to get her balance, then flew to the kitchen. She downed the rest of her 'medicine' (since she only drank to calm her nerves), and tossed the glass in the cold soapy water with the other dirty dishes.

Where did I put those mints? She splashed cold water on her face, patted it dry, and looked around for her Breathsavers. Then she remembered the ones in the cabinet behind the spices, and, wrinkling her nose, popped a couple in her mouth. Another glance at the time on her phone quickened her pace out the front door.

"Oh Lord, there's the bus!" she muttered. She jogged the short distance to the corner, feeling somewhat proud of her ability to do so, until she saw the look of disdain on the bus driver's face.

The woman motioned to little Elizabeth, who sat head down in the second row back, then said, "Sweetie, your momma's finally here. You can go now." The other three children who got off on her stop, along with their parents, had already walked down the street, but Susan didn't miss the mothers sneaking looks back at her. *Screw you!* Susan hated them and their smug attitudes. It was only then she really looked at her daughter.

"What's wrong, baby?" Susan squatted down and wiped away the tears beginning to sneak from Elizabeth's eyes. "Oh honey, it's okay. Mommy's here."

"Miss Cindy said she was taking me back to school 'cuz you weren't here." The tears flowed more freely, and she sobbed, "Why didn't you come?"

"Oh honey, I did come... I'm here now. It's okay." The words tumbled out and she hugged her child, nearly crushing the five year old. As the tears subsided, Susan looked around. She was sure there were eyes peering at them from behind every window.

Grabbing Elizabeth's hand, she half pulled, half dragged her daughter as she headed for the protection behind their front door. Elizabeth scampered along to keep up.

Once inside, Susan collapsed into a chair and watched her kindergartener drop her little backpack and flee to her bedroom. Susan knew she should probably follow and try to make up for being late to the bus stop, but the message didn't travel from her brain to her limbs.

She remembered how happy she and Marty had been five short years ago when they brought Elizabeth home from the hospital. They had marveled at the miracle lying in the pink bassinet. After years of trying, Marty had been thrilled and amazed throughout her pregnancy. He had always thought the doctors were wrong when they told him he probably would never be able to give Susan the child she wanted. But they were all wrong.

Or so he thought.

Only Susan knew better. Well, that is Susan *and* Elizabeth's real father.

Get it together! The voice of her conscience screamed at her, yet still she sat in alcohol-induced paralysis. "I'll talk to her in a little bit," she mumbled and somehow found the energy to push herself out of the chair to head for the kitchen. She would need to work up her nerve, and Susan only knew one method for nurturing courage.

She grabbed a clean glass and the bottle still sitting on the bar from earlier, poured her magic liquid and, with shaky hands, raised it to her lips. Out of the corner of her eye, she spied her daughter in the doorway, clutching her blanket, and sucking her thumb again.

CHAPTER FIVE

Val read the worry on Craig and Sarah's faces. It was a simple tonsillectomy, but—thanks to all the papers they'd signed prior to the surgery—they still worried about the 'what-ifs' and possible complications. She'd been through it all with Craig when he was about five years old, but as a grandma, even she was a bit anxious. "It shouldn't be much longer," she assured her son.

Moving to the window for a distraction, Val looked out past the rows of cars lining the visitors' parking lot to the trees beyond. Most were stubbornly holding onto their leaves of red and gold, but the impending storm would soon tear them away. It was the beginning of November, and the loss was inevitable, so Val savored the sight as she remembered her conversation with her granddaughter the night before.

"I'm not scared... but how long is it going to be before I can eat?" Mia had asked.

"Well, you'll be able to have Jello and popsicles almost right away," Val answered.

"No, I mean 'til I can really eat... like turkey and stuff."

Val had laughed at that. *"You'll be allowed a soft diet for a couple weeks, but I guarantee you'll be in good shape by the time the turkey is on the table."*

Mia had appeared relieved. Thanksgiving was such a big deal with the Reeds. Almost as exciting as Christmas... *almost.*

Val's head snapped around at the sound of the waiting room phone. Craig was the first to reach it, and Val held her breath until she saw the smile of relief on his face.

"The doctor said everything went perfectly. Mia's in recovery, and we can see her as soon as she's awake enough and they can bring her down to her room."

Val reached for her cell phone and smiled. Her first call was to Andy who'd told her to call him as soon as the surgery was over. She got his voicemail, and—since it was all good news—left a message. "Hey, Mia's in recovery. She did great, and all is well. Talk to you later."

Next, she called her best friend. "Bonnie. I'm happy to report, Mia's out of surgery and doing fine."

"Oh, good! I've been carrying my phone around all morning waiting for your call."

Val heard the relief in her friend's voice. "Yes, we're all breathing easier now. But I knew we didn't need to worry with so many prayers being said for her."

"I'll let the rest of our Bible study group know our prayers have been answered. And tell Mia I'll come see her in a day or two. I got her a book I think she'll really like... and a new sketchpad."

When Val finished her calls, she asked Craig about the other three children. He said Cody, Julie, and Bobby were doing fine with Brenda, their other grandmother, but anxious to see Mia who wouldn't be going home until tomorrow. Val was still amazed at how short the hospital stay was now compared to when Craig was a child and had the same surgery.

"Is Brenda bringing them in to see her this evening or waiting until tomorrow?" Val and Sarah's mother had become good friends since their children had married. Though they'd talked about the difficulties a blended family might have, watching the four kids together, the two women agreed this family was making it work.

"She said they couldn't wait." Craig laughed as he added, "But I told her to tell them not to give her a hard time or torment her!"

Even with family harmony, Val knew, all brothers and sisters have their moments.

When Brenda and the children arrived around 6:00, only Craig stayed in the room, grateful Madison General was so liberal with visitors in this part of the pediatric wing. Sarah and her Mom headed for the cafeteria to grab a bite.

Val had already eaten earlier, so she decided to wait there for Andy. She turned down a corridor toward the waiting room and was startled by who she ran into. Her jaw dropped at the sight of Susan Walters, and she thought about turning and going another direction... any other direction... when Susan spotted her.

"Valerie Reed! Hey, long time no see, huh?"

Val quickly tried to cover her shock at her old friend's physical appearance. She must have lost at least twenty pounds and looked dreadful. "Susan… Hi, I…um, didn't know you worked on the pediatric wing," Val said regaining her composure. "How are you?"

"I'm okay. Just switched to peds about six months ago… trying to pick up a few extra hours here and there… that's why I switched to evenings. What are you doing here?"

Val caught the odd tone in Susan's voice and wanted to end the awkward conversation as soon as possible. "My granddaughter, Mia, had a tonsillectomy this morning, and I really should go see how she's doing." She moved toward the hall leading to Mia's room, but Susan called after her.

"Is Andy here, too?"

Val's head snapped back around. "No…"

"Oh, there he is." Susan smiled and Val cursed her husband's poor timing.

Andy was hurrying toward her and obviously hadn't noticed Susan yet. From about ten feet away he began to ask how Mia was doing, then glanced at the nurse standing behind her and stopped short.

"Susan?" Before he masked his surprise, Val had seen the shock and disbelief. "Oh, wow," he said. "It's, uh, been a long time." Putting an arm around Val's shoulders he stumbled on. "I mean, how are you? How are Marty and the baby?" He glanced down at Val who was watching him curiously.

"I'm fine," Susan answered, rolling her eyes. "Marty and I are separated, and the baby isn't a baby anymore. Elizabeth is almost six years old, Andy. Where have you been?" she asked sarcastically.

Andy looked uncomfortable and embarrassed. "Oh, wow, yeah… sorry. It has been a long time." He laughed nervously and looked to Val for help.

"Well, it was good seeing you, Susan," Val lied, "but we really do need to get back to Mia."

Andy nodded in agreement and stammered something about missing his granddaughter, then guided Val down the hall in the wrong direction.

She corrected him so they had to go back past Susan who pursed her lips and followed them with her eyes.

"Well, that was awkward," Val offered when they were a safe distance away. Andy didn't respond. "Were you as surprised by her appearance as I was?" she asked.

Andy let out his breath. "What the heck happened to her? She looks like hell. I mean, like she's sick or something."

"I don't know," Val answered. *But I have an idea.*

CHAPTER SIX

Susan watched Andy and Val hurrying down the hospital corridor until they vanished from sight. Then her tough façade crumbled, and her hands shook. *Damn you both!*

"Hey Sue, the light's on for 402A. You need help?"

"No, I've got it," Susan snapped. She disliked Phyllis and took her comment as a criticism. The LPN had been getting on her nerves ever since she came on the floor. "No, I don't need your damn help," she muttered under her breath as she hastened toward room 402. *What I need is a drink!*

The little boy in 402 was recovering from leg surgery. He'd had a compound fracture after a dreadful fall out of a tree in his backyard. The child was still mildly sedated so not in pain. The only real pain—in Susan's opinion—was his mother, and she wondered what the woman *needed* this time.

"Oh good," the mother began as soon as Susan got to the door. "Can you check on Billy? His color doesn't look good, and I'm not sure… do you think his breathing sounds okay? He keeps falling back to sleep…"

"Mrs. Garner, Billy is sedated." Susan scanned his chart and dismissed his mother's concerns. "It's perfectly normal for him to sleep a lot right now. It's what his body n—"

"But I'm worried that he—" the young mother interrupted.

"Mrs. Garner," Susan snapped, "I told you he's fine!" Spying the shock on the other woman's face, she tried to soften her response. "I understand. It's hard when it's your little boy, but I assure you we're checking his vitals, and he's doing well. Now please, just try to relax. Maybe you should go get yourself a snack downstairs."

Billy's mother gawked at her, and Susan saw the hurt and anger still rising.

"I don't need anything, and I'm not leaving Billy here by himself."

"Suit yourself." Susan made a quick exit, ignoring the look of disbelief on the Garner woman's face. *I've gotta get out of here before I snap!* "I'm going down to the break room, be right back," she called over her shoulder to Phyllis as she stormed by. She didn't care what time it was or what anybody thought. She needed that drink!

Grabbing her purse out of the locker, Susan headed for the bathroom. She knew she had to be cautious. Locking the door and checking it, she took the small flask out of her bag. With shaky hands, she raised it to her lips and took a couple big gulps of the vodka, the only thing she dared drink on duty, then shuddered and waited for the trembling to stop.

One more, she thought and took another swig, then capped the flask. She knew better than to drink too much before her shift was over, but needed a little to get her through. She checked her watch. Almost 7:30. *Just a few more hours.*

♥

At 11:30 Susan was back in her car in the parking garage. She looked around, and seeing no one close, took the flask out of her handbag and drained the contents. She leaned her head back against the headrest and closed her eyes. *Just for a minute…*

Susan's head jerked up and her eyes squinted. *What the —?*

"Are you okay?" It was one of the nurses—one she didn't know well—getting off shift. "Is everything all right?"

Susan hunched her shoulders, pulled her jacket closed at the neck, trying to quiet the sudden uncontrollable shivering, and laughed nervously. "Yeah, I'm fine. Just dog-tired." She gave the younger woman a sideways look. "Thought I'd rest my eyes before heading home. Thanks!"

The young nurse didn't look convinced, but she moved on, glancing back only once.

Susan started the engine, gave her head a shake to loosen the cobwebs, and bolted out of her parking space. It would be good to get home, get rid of the sitter, and have some quiet time to herself.

And she almost made it.

She didn't even notice the flashing lights behind her until the brief sound of the siren.

"Oh shit!" *This won't turn out well.*

CHAPTER SEVEN

wo weeks after the surgery, to Val's great relief, Mia was doing fine. She was back to school and had already caught up on what she'd missed. The only ugly memory from the whole hospital experience, was their brief encounter with Susan.

Val could still remember those sunken cheeks and the dark circles under Susan's eyes. Her face looked at least fifteen to twenty years older than it had only five years earlier.

"Honestly, I was shocked when I saw her." Val took another bite of Bonnie's delicious pumpkin bread. Sitting in her best friend's kitchen, she was relieved to have a sounding board. "And you should've seen the look on Andy's face." Val looked across the table at Bonnie, knowing it was safe to confide. "I have to admit, the way he reacted to seeing her brought back uncomfortable feelings."

The line between Bonnie's eyes deepened. "You're not worried about him, are you?"

"No, no. We're good. I mean, I know there's nothing between them. Yet... I don't know how to explain it, but it was unsettling. And the way she looked at us..." Val shook her head, "I just wanted to get away from her, yanno?"

"Well, what did Andy say about it?"

Val looked at the tea in her cup and didn't answer.

"Oh Val, you mean you two haven't talked about it since you saw her? Why not?"

Still no answer. Val slowly looked up at her friend and smiled sheepishly. "Scared maybe?" At the look of incredulity on Bonnie's face, she went on. "I know it's ridiculous, but I guess I'm a little nervous about opening that whole can of worms."

"Seems to me the can is already open," Bonnie said looking over her glasses.

25

Val rolled her eyes. She knew Bonnie was right. "Yeah, I guess it is." She took a deep breath. "You're right, of course. I'm letting it stress me out when I should just talk to him. I'm sure there's nothing to worry about."

♥

Val had started the dishwasher and brought a glass of wine to Andy who was relaxing on the couch. "I had lunch at Bonnie's today," she said.

He looked up expectantly. "How is she? And how's Frank?"

"Good. I think retirement is agreeing with her." Val smiled remembering how difficult the decision to retire had been for Bonnie who loved her college students. But she had finally decided her husband was her priority, and she wanted to spend as much time as possible with him for as long as she could. "She said Frank is much better. He was thrilled to finally be able to hit a golf ball again." Bonnie's husband had feared he might never play again after his second stroke. It was a lot worse than the first one, but through sheer will-power, he had regained full use of his left arm and leg, even though he didn't have the feeling back. "He was determined, and he hardly uses his cane at all now. Still, Bonnie worries."

"Yeah, I guess that's understandable. She's been through it twice. Scary stuff."

"That's why she finally retired." Val took a sip of her wine and looked at her husband. "She's afraid of losing him." Andy nodded, but Val wondered if he had any idea she worried about the same thing. She wasn't as sure of herself now as she recently had been. "Andy, I've been meaning to talk to you about something." Val's mouth went dry. She took another sip of wine before answering his raised eyebrows. "You know when we ran into Susan at the hospital?" Her husband nodded ever so slowly. "Well, I just wondered what you thought."

"I thought she looked like hell," he answered quickly. "Like she's been sick or something."

"Do you think it might be because she and Marty separated?"

"Yeah, could be. That was a shocker, wasn't it?" Andy put his glass down and shook his head.

Val hesitated before responding. "Well, actually, Kathy mentioned something about it at bridge club a month ago."

"Oh?" Andy's eyebrows shot up, and he leaned forward. "How come you never mentioned it?"

"Why should I?" She heard the edge in her own voice and hurried on, grinning. "I mean, you know how Kathy gossips. If I told you every story she tells when we play cards, I'd talk your ear off." She knew Andy saw right through her. "And, well, I guess Susan was just a topic I didn't have any desire to pursue."

Andy lowered his eyes. "I'm sorry," he muttered.

"No, no, I didn't mean it that way. I didn't mean to make you feel bad. Jeeze, that's ancient history!" This was not what she'd expected. But then she hadn't really known what to expect. "It's just my own insecurities." Val knew he blamed himself for that too, and it took a while to reassure him. Now she wasn't sure if she should go on, but she plunged ahead. "There was actually more to the rumor, and after seeing her, I'm wondering if there might be some truth in it."

"Like what?"

"Kathy said she thought something else was wrong. And last week she told us her brother-in-law, who's a cop, said Susan got stopped for drunk driving on the way home from the hospital one night."

"What the hell?" Andy said incredulously. "That doesn't sound like the Susan I knew… I mean… the Susan *we both knew*. I thought she and Marty were over the moon once they had the baby." Andy stood and started pacing. "She had what she wanted. Why the hell would she screw it up?"

Val wasn't sure what kind of reaction she'd expected, but it wasn't this. Why was he reacting so strongly? She wished she didn't know the answer, but a sick feeling in the pit of her stomach said she did. "Andy, what's going on with you? Come sit down and talk to me."

He quickly did as she asked. "Sweetheart, I'm sorry. But if Marty is out of the picture, well, what if she really is messed up? Who's watching out for the baby?"

"Elizabeth is not a baby anymore, remember?" Val asked. She couldn't help the growing agitation she was experiencing. "She's got to be—what did Susan say—yeah, five years old."

"That may be, but I don't think a five year old is beyond needing care." Andy was on his feet again.

"And I don't think that's your concern!" Val said sharply. She regretted the words as soon as they were out of her mouth. She saw the instant look of hurt in her husband's eyes. After an agonizing five seconds, she jumped up and ran into his arms. "I'm sorry. That was mean. But we don't know what's really going on."

Andy wrapped his arms around her and the two stood in forgiving silence laden with anxiety. Neither wanted to say what both were thinking.

What if Elizabeth was not being cared for? What if she was in danger?

What if Elizabeth was really Andy's child?

CHAPTER EIGHT

Susan's nails bit into her palms as she glared out the window at the car she couldn't drive. It was bad enough she'd lost her license, but now she'd lost her job. Life had been in a downward spiral ever since the night she got the DWI, and she blamed everybody—that is everyone but herself.

She had been managing before Madison General found out she'd been stopped for drunk driving. Before that patient's mother, Mrs. Garner, complained about her not caring about the children she was charged to care for. Before they realized she was drinking while on duty. Before they knew she was a drunk.

Now Susan sat in her house hour after hour, often with the curtains drawn, sinking in a quagmire of self-pity. Angry at the world and everyone in it—even the most innocent—she lashed out. Elizabeth often felt the sting of her mother's sharp tongue. The child would cower and cry, intensifying Susan's guilt-ridden anger.

"What is *wrong* with you?" she'd shout at the child, who would cry harder.

In her most lucid moments, Susan was concerned that Elizabeth spent more and more time alone in her room. But just as often, she was relieved that the child seemed content to live in her private world of imagination. When hungry, Elizabeth would venture out, and, if she was lucky, her mom would be coherent enough to talk to.

"Momma?" Elizabeth said in a half whisper.

Susan looked up from her glass.

"I'm hungry."

This was one of Susan's better days. She pushed herself to a standing position and staggered to the kitchen while her five year old watched. A few minutes later Elizabeth was content to be eating her peanut butter sandwich. She even had a big glass of milk although she said it tasted a little funny.

Susan stood guiltily watching her daughter for a few minutes, then turned to leave.

"Aren't you going to eat too, Momma?" Elizabeth asked hopefully.

"No, honey. Momma's not hungry."

"But you can sit with me," the child said hopefully, looking into her mother's bloodshot eyes.

Susan reached for the chair across the table from her daughter. "Okay, sweetie." She saw the surprised pleasure on Elizabeth's face and instantly resented it. "Hurry up and eat your sandwich."

Elizabeth took a really big bite, probably because of what Susan had said. But it was too big. The peanut butter jammed in her mouth and gagged her. She heaved so hard she choked. Her eyes filled with terror and Susan jumped out of her seat, rushing around the table.

Susan pounded Elizabeth on the back while the child desperately tried to swallow, to no avail. The whole gummy mess wound up on her plate, along with her tears.

As she gasped for breath, she looked up at her mother.

Weeping, Susan pulled Elizabeth out of the chair, and drew her close. *Oh my God, oh my God!* She clutched the child tightly to her chest.

"Momma, you're hurting me," Elizabeth said.

Susan loosened her grip. "I'm sorry, baby, I'm so sorry." She stroked her hair, and repeated, "I'm sorry, baby."

"It's okay, Momma. You didn't mean it. I'm okay," Elizabeth comforted her mother.

Susan swept the mess away and went for her phone. She called in an order for a medium pizza, glad she still had her credit card to pay for it. "Come here, baby. Sit on Momma's lap." She knew Elizabeth hated the alcohol smell on her breath, but loved being held. Susan could see the child's conflict and hated herself for not being a better mother… the kind of mother she used to be.

I'll do better, Elizabeth, she thought. *Starting tomorrow, I'll do better.*

And she meant it… when she said it.

The next day started out a little rough, but Susan remembered the promise she'd made to herself the night before. She resolved to keep that promise in spite of how horrible she felt. She dragged herself out of bed, brushed her teeth—twice—and looked up in the mirror in disgust. "You are a mess, Susan Walters!" It took her a little longer than usual, but she managed to shower, dress, and pull a comb through her hair without taking a drink.

She was feeling a little shaky when she went in to wake her daughter up for school, but at least she was present today.

After smelling the milk, she poured it down the drain. "How about waffles for breakfast?"

Elizabeth grinned and nodded.

Susan put two frozen waffles into the toaster, and when they popped up, put one on each of their plates. Elizabeth would have to settle for water to drink, but she didn't seem to mind at all. The child was happy all the way to the bus stop.

Susan felt the other three mothers sneaking glances at her. Oh, they were all polite. They said good morning, then quickly turned their attention back to their children.

You can all kiss my ass, Susan thought. Fortunately, the bus was right on time. Susan kissed her daughter goodbye and waved as it pulled away, but she hadn't missed the judgmental look from the bus driver either. *And you can kiss my ass, too!*

Back in the house Susan looked around. The place could certainly do with a little cleaning, but when she reached under the sink to get the Lysol her hands were trembling. She stood looking out the window then slammed the cleaner down and grabbed her car keys and purse.

After two steps toward the garage, she remembered she'd lost her license.

In utter exasperation, she dropped her purse and threw the keys across the room. *It's not fair!* Tears of frustration streamed down her face. Hopelessly trapped, the need to do something was driving her to act, but how? She flung open cupboards and the refrigerator, grabbing whatever she could find.

It was thirty-five minutes later when she looked at the mountain of empty cereal boxes, candy wrappers, and ice cream cartons and wept harder. She would have to clean up this mess... destroy the evidence, call her order for replacements in for delivery... *I can't let Elizabeth see this*. But before she even started, there was something else she had to do.

Susan slowly made her way to the bathroom, got on her knees, and purged.

When it was over, she sat leaning against the side of the bathtub. She wiped her face and neck with a wet washcloth and opened the front of her shirt. Sweat dripped down the sides of her face, as the floor tilted beneath her feet. Holding onto the sink for balance with one hand, she held the other one out in front of her and watched it shake uncontrollably. *What are you doing?*

Sitting there, Susan thought about how much her life had changed in the past year. She remembered how the glass of wine she used to have for dinner had become two... and then three. She remembered how Marty started getting on her case about the drinking, until she started hiding it from him and everyone else. Perhaps he had never really been sure of her eating disorder, but he certainly knew she drank and hated what it did to her.

Susan remembered the night she had too much to drink and they argued. They had argued before, but this time it went too far. Marty accused her of being a neglectful mother. He threatened to take Elizabeth and leave her.

That's when she snapped.

"Don't you dare!" she had screamed at him. He ignored her, turned his back on her, and moved toward the closet. Susan wouldn't let him take her child. *"You can't take my baby!"* she'd cried.

"She's our baby," he responded.

Without thinking Susan blurted, *"No! She's MY baby! She's not yours!"*

Marty had stopped and turned to look at her, his expression gradually morphing from anger to disbelief to sheer pain. Somehow he must've known in that moment it was true. Yet he asked, *"What are you saying, Susan?"*

She would always wonder if she could have repaired the damage by lying, but she was too drunk at the time. It all came tumbling out.

Then it was over. It didn't matter how much she cried or what she said, he was done… and then he was gone. And, somehow, Elizabeth slept through it all.

Now, alone, Susan's addictions had spiraled out of control, and she didn't know how to stop it. She wasn't sure she even wanted to. *But I have to, for Elizabeth.*

The child had asked about her father nearly every day at first. She couldn't understand how her daddy could suddenly not be there. He'd come to see her a few times, took her for ice cream, and even told her how much he loved her. But then he'd leave.

"I'm sorry, punkin," he'd said the last time, *"but Daddy has to go work in another town far away for a while."*

Susan remembered how her daughter had cried herself to sleep that night, and nothing she said could take away the hurt in Elizabeth's eyes. How could she explain? It was impossible.

My nerves are a wreck. She walked back to the living room and over to the liquor cabinet. *I'll just have one… to calm my nerves.*

CHAPTER NINE

Val's fingertips whitened as she gripped the unopened letter. Resisting the urge to rip it open, she stared at the return address then dropped it like a hot potato. It was not addressed to her. It was addressed to Andy. Ordinarily a piece of mail addressed to her husband would get tossed on the kitchen desk without a second thought, but the sender's name sent a chill up her spine and made her tremble.

It was from Marty Walters.

Retrieving the unopened envelope, Val gingerly placed it where it *belonged,* turned her back on the worrisome missive, and reached for her phone. She needed the counsel of a friend in this moment of temptation and dread. Bonnie could talk her off the ledge.

Since Frank had gone to try nine holes of golf, Bonnie invited Val to join her for an early lunch. "It won't be anything fancy… just tuna and talk."

"Are you sure? I mean that sounds great to me if you're sure you have enough." Val needed to get out of the house and away from the temptation to open Andy's letter. "I'll be right over."

She slipped into her coat, grabbed her keys off the hook, and with one final glance at the letter, hurried out to the car.

Fifteen minutes later, Val was being led to the breakfast nook off Bonnie's kitchen. She was impressed, though not surprised, to see how lovely the table looked, and the aroma of fresh baked bread was somehow comforting.

"You are the quintessential hostess, for sure."

"Oh, it's easy when you're retired," the older woman laughed, but Val remembered and knew entertaining and being the perfect homemaker seemed second nature to Bonnie Dixon. She and Frank were unpretentious, yet had a grace that lent itself to stress-free entertaining and making each of their guests feel warm and welcomed.

Today's spur of the moment luncheon was laid out with such charm and flair, Val nearly forgot what had brought her here. That is until Bonnie sat down across from her and asked, "So what's going on, dear? Or would you rather eat first and talk later?"

Val met Bonnie's eyes and knew she would understand. "I think we can eat and talk at the same time." Val smiled and took a sip of tea. "You know how Kathy said Susan and Marty have separated... and I told you about how awful Sue looked when we ran into her at the hospital?"

Bonnie nodded.

"Well, it sort of stirred up all that stuff from back when Andy and I were having our problems and he..." it was hard for her to even say the words, "when he had his affair with her."

"But you and Andy got past that," Bonnie said. She sat back in her chair then leaned forward again. "Your marriage is as solid now as any I've ever seen. You're not worried about Andy seeing Susan again, are you?" she asked incredulously.

"No! No, not at all. You're right, we've never been better."

Val had confided in Bonnie when Susan turned up pregnant so soon after her affair with Andy... but obviously Bonnie thought the worries had ended with the baby's adorable strawberry blond hair. Val's husband didn't have red hair... but Marty did.

What she had never shared with Bonnie until now, was their shock a few months later at the funeral of Andy's Uncle Stu... when they saw a cousin—a little boy—with that same strawberry blond hair. Some digging into their genealogy uncovered an ancestor by the name of Margaret Riley who was described as having a temper befitting a woman with such flaming red hair.

Bringing Bonnie up to date seemed to lessen the burden for Val. She looked across the table and saw the look of shock turn to concern.

"Oh Val, I'm so sorry. But after all this time, why are you telling me this now? I mean, I understand why you never mentioned it before, but why now?"

Yes indeed, why now?

"Is it because Sue and Marty aren't together? Do you think she might say something? Or does she even suspect Andy is the father?"

"I don't know what she thinks, Bonnie." Val picked up her half-eaten sandwich and put it down again. "No, what I didn't tell you is what came in the mail today. There was a letter. For Andy. From *Marty*."

Bonnie gasped, "Do you think—"

"I don't know what to think," Val interrupted, "but why would Marty suddenly write to Andy? What else could it possibly be about?"

"So you didn't open it?" Bonnie interjected.

Val shook her head.

"Good for you. I know that must have been difficult. Does Andy know about it yet?"

"No, he's with clients, and it's not a message I'd want to leave on his voicemail. I have to admit, I was tempted to rip the envelope open. I can hardly stand waiting." Val laughed nervously. "Coming here served two purposes—lunch with my best friend, and removing myself from temptation."

The two friends finished lunch, cleaned up the few dishes, and retired to the family room to continue their conversation.

"So Val, what if you determine Elizabeth is Andy's child? What happens then? Does it change anything for you?"

"I don't know, Bonnie. I just don't know." She checked the time. "You know what? Andy will probably be home soon, and I want to be there when he finds the letter so I'd better get going."

Bonnie hugged her a little tighter and longer than usual, said goodbye, and told her to call if she needed to talk.

Back in her car, Val wondered, *What if it's true? What will happen?* She had lots of questions but absolutely no answers.

CHAPTER TEN

Val sat curled up next to her husband on the couch. He had one arm around her shoulders and held the opened letter on his lap with the other hand. Neither of them had spoken for several minutes. But it was all right.

"Val?" he finally said.

"Hmm?"

"What are we going to do now?"

Suddenly Val wasn't so sure everything was okay. "I don't know, sweetheart." She turned and looked up at him, saw the deep crease in his brow, and knew he was worried about the child. "What are you thinking?"

In the letter, Marty had revealed more than the fact that Elizabeth was not his daughter. He'd also disclosed Susan's drinking problem and his concern for the child's well-being. Marty said he loved the little girl he had raised for five years, yet he knew he couldn't gain custody in a court of law. Susan had gotten a blood test to prove paternity and threw it in his face. He revealed that she had screamed, *"You'll never take her away from me!"*

The final straw, and the reason Marty had decided to write to Andy, was when he learned she had lost her license for driving under the influence. She had called him to ask for help taking Elizabeth to the pediatrician for a check-up and had to confess.

"This letter confirms my worst fears. If Marty wasn't still sending them money for groceries and childcare, God knows what would happen." Andy hesitated before going on. "I think I need to go see them."

Val sat up straighter and turned so she could see her husband's face clearly. *"Them?"* she asked.

"Susan and Elizabeth."

"Why? I mean, what are you going to do?"

39

"I don't know, Val. But I need to see for myself… I need to be sure she's okay. Elizabeth, I mean." He took his wife's hand in his. "Do you want to come with me?"

Val thought about it for a moment. "No, I think this is something you need to do alone… unless you want me to come?"

She felt him squeeze her hand reassuringly, and he shook his head. "I guess it would be better if I do this on my own. Are you sure you're okay with it?"

How could she not be? They were talking about his child.

And then it hit her.

"Oh my gosh, Andy. Craig has a sister, a baby sister!"

Val's eyes welled unexpectedly. Craig had never known the sister he had in heaven, the daughter they'd lost at birth. But now he had a half-sister… one who was years younger than his own children. She wondered how he would take the news. Or if they should even tell him.

She looked up at Andy and voiced the question.

After a short pause, he responded, "Let's cross that bridge when we come to it."

♥

Val poured her third cup of coffee, added sweetener and creamer, and stirred it absently. She carried it to her office, looked at the laptop on her desk, and changed her mind. There was no way she would be able to concentrate on the human-interest story she was working on right now. She walked to the front of the house and pulled back the curtain to peer down the street.

Coffee still in hand, she meandered around, looking at the pictures on the walls. Her gaze stopped at the frames where her two favorite pictures hung side by side. The first 16" x 20" was of her son Craig with his beautiful first wife, Jenny, and their two children, Mia and Cody. Her grandchildren were only three and four years old in that picture, and they all looked so happy. The drunk driver responsible for the crash that shortly thereafter killed Jenny was nothing but a kid himself—nineteen years old—and his actions had devastated so many lives.

Val sighed, still feeling the loss, then her eyes moved to the portrait hung next to it and a smile crept across her face. It was another picture of Craig but with a much bigger family now. He and his wife, Sarah, sat side by side with Mia, Cody, and Sarah's children, Julie and Bobby Jr. It was a picture of a man and woman who had each tragically lost their spouse yet survived and learned to love again. It was a blended family that seemed to work, in spite of how difficult that can be, because of the love.

Four beautiful grandchildren, Val thought. *We really are blessed.*

To her relief, she heard the garage door opening. Andy was home at last. He hadn't really been gone that long, but it seemed like an eternity. Rather than run into the kitchen to meet him, Val quickly took a seat on the end of the couch and placed her coffee on the coaster on the end table to her left.

Andy came directly to the family room where he knew she'd be waiting. One look at his face, and Val knew it wasn't good. She patted the seat next to her, inviting him to join her, which he did. Val exhaled, only just realizing she'd been holding her breath. "Well, how did it go? Did you get to talk to her, and was the child there?"

"Yes, and yes. Elizabeth was there, but Susan sent her into her bedroom while we talked."

Val waited expectantly for him to continue but was ready to ask more questions.

"She looks awful, Val, and she's definitely been drinking." He dropped his head, stared at the floor, and looked back up into his wife's eyes. "It's not good."

CHAPTER ELEVEN

Susan peeked into her daughter's bedroom and watched the child playing with her favorite toys—Fisher Price's Little People. Since Elizabeth appeared content, Susan quietly backed out and leaned against the wall. She needed more time to get herself together.

Seeing Andy again had been unsettling. She had put him out of her mind and barely ever thought about him at all after Elizabeth was born. Well, except sometimes when her husband was making love to her and she fantasized that it was Andy.

So, when she'd opened the door and found herself face to face with him in her own home, Susan's stomach had flipped. It wasn't that bad when she'd run into him and Val at the hospital that night. Of course, she had seen Val first and kind of braced herself before he showed up.

But today he caught her totally by surprise. And she didn't like it.

She pushed off the wall and went straight to the liquor cabinet. "I don't know who he thinks he is showing up here giving me the third degree," she muttered. "Screw you, Andy Reed! I don't need you or your pity." She filled her glass with vodka, not even bothering with ice, and took a couple of big gulps.

"Momma."

Susan jumped at the unexpected voice behind her.

"I'm hungry, Momma. Are we gonna have lunch soon?"

"It's only…" Susan looked at her watch and was surprised to see it was 2:15. "Oh, yeah, okay. Let's get you something to eat." Turning too quickly, she had to grab hold of the counter to catch her balance.

"Are you okay, Momma?" Elizabeth whispered.

"Of course I'm okay," Susan snapped back.

She managed to get her daughter a cold cheese sandwich and a glass of milk but was glad to sit down when she was done. This was proving to be a very difficult day.

Elizabeth ate in silence, glancing cautiously up every few seconds.

Susan watched her daughter chew and chew and chew until she couldn't stand it for one more second. She groaned and pushed herself away from the table and went to refill her glass.

She didn't see Elizabeth stuff the rest of her sandwich into her tiny mouth until she almost choked. She didn't see the tears that slid down the child's cheeks. She didn't really see much of anything as she stared into space. Susan was lost in thoughts of how her life had become so terrible, how everyone was against her, and how unfair the world was in general.

She thought about the mother she had learned to hate. Nothing she ever did was good enough for her. *I tried so hard. I always made honor roll... well... at least until junior year, but you wanted to know why I didn't have all A's.* Susan had finally given up trying to please her mother and instead started doing the opposite. Her grades went from A's and B's to near failing, and by her senior year, she managed to graduate only by the skin of her teeth. And she simply didn't care.

"Oh God, I can't be that kind of mother to Elizabeth." She realized she had spoken out loud and looked around to see if her daughter was listening. Luckily the child wasn't in the room. Susan was alone in the kitchen.

Though not yet six years old, Elizabeth was already becoming a little helper. Her plate and cup were in the dishwasher, her napkin in the trash, but the girl had vanished into her room again.

Susan was tempted to leave well enough alone and just go lie down, but remembering her own mother, she had one of those rare moments of conscience that said she should check on her.

Elizabeth's door was closed but not so tight that Susan couldn't peek in. She saw her daughter sitting on the floor in the middle of many toys, especially dolls and Little People. Her back was to the door as she held two of her dolls, one in each hand. It was obvious the two were having a conversation.

Susan smiled and was about to move away when she heard something she wasn't expecting.

"I said hurry up. You take too long. No. Stop dawdling and eat," said the blonde Barbie in an angry voice. Elizabeth shook the smaller baby doll and replied softer, "But Mommy, I can't." Then her voice changed back and said, "Yes, you can. Now hurry up!" Elizabeth shook the Barbie at the other one as if threatening her.

Susan's jaw dropped, and she pushed the door open. "Elizabeth! What are you doing?" she yelled incredulously.

The child jumped and spun around. She looked at her mother then down at the floor. "I'm sorry."

Susan was sure the child didn't even know what she was saying she was sorry about. She simply stared in disbelief… dumbfounded… not knowing how to respond.

She finally realized her child was frightened. "Princess," Susan said softly, "you didn't do anything wrong. It's okay."

Her daughter visibly relaxed at the sound of the pet name she rarely heard anymore.

"Momma just didn't know what you were playing, that's all." She smiled feebly, but the room was beginning to sway. "It's okay. You play. I'm just going to go lie down for a little while, okay?"

Elizabeth nodded and turned back to her dolls.

Susan managed to make it to her bedroom, collapsed on the bed, and slipped into a drunken stupor.

It was dark when Elizabeth tried to wake her mother. It had been hours since she'd eaten that cheese sandwich, and her stomach was hurting. She tapped her mother's shoulder timidly until she finally roused her.

"What?" Susan asked groggily. "What do you want, Elizabeth?"

"I'm hungry, Momma," she whispered.

"Again? But you just ate!"

Elizabeth didn't reply. She stood quietly by the bed until she saw her mother had gone back to sleep.

She tiptoed out of the room and went to the kitchen. In desperation, she pushed a stool over to the kitchen counter, climbed up and managed to reach a box of Cheerios. There wasn't any more milk in the refrigerator, so she sat down on the kitchen floor, reached in the box, and grabbed a handful, stuffing it into her mouth.

♥

Susan woke sometime during the night to use the bathroom. Her head hurt and her mouth was sour. Her stomach growled. She stumbled to the bathroom, peed and got a drink of water. She didn't remember even going to bed.

Before heading to the bedroom, she went to the kitchen for something to eat. That's where she found her Elizabeth—a handful of Cheerios held loosely on her chest—sound asleep on the kitchen floor.

Gently lifting the child into her arms, Susan carried her to bed and covered her with a blanket. And tears.

CHAPTER TWELVE

Val was glad this Thursday's bridge game was at Bonnie's house, but not merely because she loved the warmth and hospitality of the Dixon home. She had asked Bonnie if she could come early and help set up, but she had more on her mind than helping her friend get ready.

"What's going on, Val? What's wrong?" Bonnie hung her coat in the closet then turned and pulled her in for a hug.

"Wow, nothing gets by you, does it?" Val asked, accepting the hug and returning it.

When she pulled back, Val was surprised by the tears threatening to escape and run down her face. She quickly blinked them back.

Bonnie grabbed a tissue from the pack she kept in her pocket and handed it to her. She waited quietly for Val to regain her composure before leading her into the next room. Sitting side by side on the soft leather sofa, Bonnie took both of Val's hands in hers. "Something has obviously upset you. What can I do?"

"I'm sorry, Bonnie. I'm such a mess."

Bonnie gently brushed the hair back from Val's eyes, then lifted her chin to make eye contact. Val saw the depth of concern hidden there and knew she was right to confide in her friend.

"It's Susan. I told you about us running into her at the hospital and then hearing from Marty. Well…" she sighed, "the letter told us things were worse than we thought. Apparently, Susan has been drinking a lot, and Marty thinks she has a real problem." Val looked down at her hands, then back up at Bonnie. "And he's worried about their little girl."

"I'm so sorry to hear that."

Val nodded in understanding. She had been sorry to hear it, too. But what concerned her more was Andy. "There's more. Marty confirmed that Elizabeth is not his biological child."

Bonnie's jaw dropped.

"I guess they had a big fight one night when Susan had been drinking a lot. When he threatened to take Elizabeth and leave, she blurted it out." There was a pause and Val pulled her hand back through her hair. "Marty said in his letter she told him about her affair with Andy, how she'd lied about having to work and met him for their secret rendezvous." Val couldn't help the bitterness in her voice. "Bonnie, you should have seen Andy's face after reading that."

Her breath caught. "Oh, my dear girl, what can I do? How can I help?"

Val offered a weak smile. "I just needed a friend I could talk to about all of this, and I knew I could count on you."

"Of course… always!"

Val was sure Bonnie wanted to say more, to ask more, but they heard a car pull into the driveway.

"Oh dear, I was hoping they wouldn't be early tonight."

Val knew Bonnie didn't normally mind at all.

"Can you stay for a little while after the game?" she asked hurriedly.

Val nodded. "I'm going to run into the bathroom quick while you get the door." She took a few minutes to compose herself then returned wearing a cheerful smile and greeted Sarah and Kathy. She didn't miss the brief quizzical look on her daughter-in-law's face.

The cards fell well for Sarah and Kathy who thoroughly enjoyed their easy wins. It wasn't too often they were victorious over their opponents. There was lots of chatting and laughter, and much to Val's relief, no one mentioned Susan Walters.

At the end of the evening, Val lingered behind as Kathy left and Sarah gathered her coat and bag. "Are you ready to go, Val?" Sarah didn't refer to her mother-in-law as 'Mom' the way Jenny had. She was 'Val' or 'Grandma' to her.

"No, you go ahead, hon. I need to talk to Bonnie about alter guild for a few minutes before I leave." She gave Sarah a hug and told her she would see her Sunday. "Don't forget, dinner is at our house this week."

Sarah laughed. "Don't worry! I always look forward to the Sundays I don't have to cook."

Alone again, Bonnie signaled for Val to sit down and asked if she wanted another cup of tea.

"No thanks, I've got my water." She looked at her long-time friend in anticipation. She knew there would be questions.

"Okay, tell me to shut up if I ask too much, but what's going on?"

Val put her glass on the coaster and turned to face Bonnie. In painful, slow sentences she revealed all that had transpired during Andy's visit to Susan's house.

"Andy said he could tell Susan had been drinking a lot, and Elizabeth was there. When he said the child's name, I saw something in his eyes." Val looked up at Bonnie. "It's all so crazy. I mean, what if he wants to be part of her life?"

Bonnie took a deep breath. "Do you think that's what's going on? I mean, did he say that?"

"Well, no... not yet. But Bonnie, you should have seen his face! Now that he knows Elizabeth is his daughter, I'm afraid Susan's going to suck him back in." She looked helplessly up at her friend desperate for some kind of help... some kind of reassurance.

"Val!" Bonnie said sharply. "You listen to me. Andy loves you, right?"

Val nodded as a tear slipped out of the corner of her eye and down the side of her nose.

"And you love him?"

Val nodded again.

"Then you're going to be all right."

"But how? What should I do?"

Her friend responded by taking her hands again and adding, "Trust in the Lord."

That was all she said, but it was enough. Val knew she was right. "I'll try to remember that." She smiled sheepishly. "But it's easy to forget when life gets crazy—and believe me, this is crazy."

"I know, child. It's easy to say the words. A lot harder to live it every day." She glanced toward the study where Frank was probably reading, or asleep with a book in front of him, and added, "I certainly have my own moments of doubt and fear, especially since his second stroke."

Val suddenly remembered. "I'm sorry, I guess you have enough on your plate without me adding to your worries."

"Don't be silly. That's what friends are for." Bonnie squeezed her hand then looked back toward the study as Frank walked in.

"Oh, Val, I didn't know you were still here," he said.

"Hi, Frank. Yes," Val said getting to her feet, "but I'm leaving now."

"Don't run out on my account, dear. You girls can visit as long as you want. I'm just getting some water."

"I know, Frank, but it's getting late, and I don't want Andy to worry." She glanced meaningfully at Bonnie. "I'll see you Sunday morning… and thanks."

After a final hug, Val slipped into her car and headed home. Talking with her friend had been reassuring, and she felt more in control than she had since reading the return address on the letter from Marty.

She was much calmer. That is, until she hit the automatic garage door opener and it opened to an empty garage. Andy's car was gone.

CHAPTER THIRTEEN

"Wow, are all the kids settled already?" Sarah's eyebrows shot up before she took note of the time. "Oh, no wonder. I didn't realize we got done so late tonight. I guess it took Kathy and I a little longer than usual to *win* it all tonight."

"Do I detect a wee bit of gloating?"

Craig set his book aside to give her his full attention. That's one of the things she loved about him.

"You and your partner are making a habit of winning lately, aren't you? Keep that up and Bonnie and Mom might kick you out of the group," Craig teased.

"Trust me, it won't become a habit. Although Kathy's bidding is really improving." Sarah snuggled up next to Craig who was sitting in his usual spot at the end of the sectional. "I actually think a lot of the credit tonight goes to your mom."

Craig looked puzzled. "What does that mean?"

"That means, she really seemed to be off her game this evening. She trumped her partner's trick *twice*. Oh, and one hand, Bonnie bid four hearts—and really had the cards—but Mom jumped to five clubs, and they went down." Sarah rolled her eyes and chuckled, "It's a good thing Bonnie doesn't care that much about winning or losing." Sarah gave her husband a quick peck on the cheek and sprang from her spot on the couch. "Don't go 'way. I'm gonna go look in on the kids. I wouldn't be upset if I found a glass of chardonnay when I get back," she called over her shoulder.

Craig didn't let her down. Sarah found him holding out a glass of her favorite wine when she returned a few minutes later. "Are they all sleeping?" he asked.

"Just about. Mia was working in her sketchbook, but she agreed she'd better get to sleep since it's a school night. And Julie had fallen asleep reading. The boys were both out cold."

"Do you wanna watch some TV?" Craig reached for the remote but Sarah shook her head.

"No, not really. Let's just chill, okay?"

"You got it, angel." Sarah smiled at the sound of his pet name for her. They sat quietly sipping wine for a while chatting about their days, but she caught herself yawning even before she'd drained her glass.

"Hmm, looks like you're ready for bed." Obviously Craig had noticed, too. "Here, let me take your glass and we'll head on back."

They both loved having their master suite on the main floor in the new house, and waking up to the view of their pool and the greenspace beyond.

But right now, Sarah wasn't thinking about the view of anything but her hunky husband, and before long she was under the covers waiting for him. "All of a sudden, I'm not so sleepy," she murmured when he climbed in next to her.

"Oh yeah? Is that right?" Craig faked a yawn. "Well, I don't know. I'm getting kind of drowsy."

Sarah pulled out one of the pillows and swatted him on the head... just before he pinned her down, and their muffled laughter melted into unspoken passion.

Later, as she was drifting off to sleep, Sarah was surprised to feel her husband roll over and put his arm around her.

"I love you," he whispered so softly she barely heard the words.

Sarah sighed and slipped into a peaceful sleep with a smile on her lips.

♥

Breakfast could be rather chaotic in the young Reed household, with four children vying for attention. Too often, Sarah found permission slips, assignments, and other school papers being thrust in her face for signatures while she was trying to caffeinate. "It's a good thing I like iced coffee," she often joked.

This morning was no exception. Cody and Bobby's bickering began to grate on her nerves as she was dealing with another last-minute envelope. "Cody, Bobby, stop! And why didn't you tell me they were doing the hockey team pictures today?"

She loved that they were doing the same sport and she made it to as many games as possible—especially on the days Craig couldn't make it—but she was amazed that neither one of them seemed responsible enough to give her a heads-up on things like this.

"I said stop." That was when she felt an arm go around her waist and a deep familiar voice come to her aid.

"You heard her. No? Okay, three minutes silent time for the boys." Craig set the timer and Cody immediately clammed up.

Sarah saw Bobby open his mouth to protest, but seeing his mother's warning look, closed it again and just scowled.

"Oh good, now *we* can talk," Julie said.

Mia laughed at the wrath written on both the boys' faces. "Don't antagonize your brothers." But even she was anxious to get a few words in while they enjoyed the luxury of Cody and Bobby's silence. "Craig, these guys get their team pictures today. Do you care which package I order?"

"You'd better get the biggest one. You know the grands will want copies, too." He looked at the boys who were watching the timer count down. "Yes, your time's about up, but don't start right up again, or you know what's next."

Cody and Bobby exchanged side-long glances that spoke agreement. Neither of them wanted the *ten* minutes of no talking that they knew would be the next step.

Sarah finished filling out the forms, put money in the envelopes and tossed them to the boys. "Put these in your backpacks now before you go off and leave them here."

The boys grabbed the envelopes and headed back to their rooms to get their stuff.

"Hey, get back here," Craig called. They turned back looking confused. "It's the maid's day off."

Grinning sheepishly, they took the reminder to put their cereal bowls in the sink, and their sisters followed suit.

When all four children had gone to finish getting ready in time to catch the school bus, Sarah heaved an exaggerated sigh of relief. "And we want another one of those?" she laughed.

"Yeah, are you sure about this?" Craig asked in all sincerity. "With four pre-teens, and a new baby it's going to be a lot."

Sarah smiled. "Yes, call me crazy… but I'm sure." She put her arms around her husband's neck, and with a secret smile added, "besides, it might be a little late to reconsider now."

CHAPTER FOURTEEN

Susan sat in the back of the police car. In and out of consciousness. Confused. Rousing, she jumped, became aware of her surroundings... and lost control.

"What? What the hell? Hey!" she yelled in a panic. "Hey you, where's my daughter? Where's my little girl?" she shrieked.

An officer opened the front door of the squad car and leaned in. "Calm down, lady. Your little girl is fine... no thanks to you," he barked.

"Where is she? What did you do with Elizabeth?"

"Hey, there's no sense getting hysterical. I told you she's okay. But you're not. Now, who can we call for you?"

"What? What do you mean?" Susan rubbed her head in confusion. "How did I get here? What happened?"

"You were in an accident—ran your car into that tree. You're lucky you weren't going any faster."

Susan felt the bile in her throat. Panic-stricken she stretched her neck trying to see, trying to find Elizabeth, but those flashing lights were blinding. She couldn't see anything but those glaring lights. "Please, I need to see my little girl," she cried.

"I'm sorry, ma'am. That isn't possible right now. They have her in the ambulance..."

"What? Ambulance? Is she hurt? Oh my God, is she okay?"

The officer quickly assured her the child was fine. They were just checking her out. They were in fact, also trying to calm her down. "Now, ma'am, who can we call?"

"I don't know what you mean. Why do you need to call anyone?"

"We need someone to come get the child. We're going to check her out over at Madison General, but then should we call your husband to come pick her up?"

"No!" Susan felt the skin prickle on the back of her neck. This was wrong. Why wouldn't they let her see Elizabeth? She begged and pleaded with the officer until he finally got through to her. She wasn't going home. She'd be spending the night in jail. Susan began to sober up. *What have I done?*

"My husband is… *gone.* Call Andrew Reed," she finally said. "Call Dr. Andrew Reed. He's her father."

♥

Andy ended the call and sat down, knees shaking. Even after sitting, his right knee bounced up and down madly, as if it had a mind of its own. He had just gotten home from a quick visit with his son, Craig, and four grandchildren. In the last five years, he had grown to love his two step-grandchildren just like his biological two. Andy loved spending time with the kids. He loved being a grandfather. But now, in an instant, he was being called on to be the father of a daughter he'd never met.

The officer on the phone obviously assumed he would come and get the child right away. Andy was dumbfounded.

"What choice do I have?" he muttered.

Breaking out of his temporary paralysis, he mechanically crossed the room, grabbed his keys, and headed to the garage. As he backed out of the driveway, he hesitated, unable to think clearly. He'd been to Madison General many times yet now his brain failed him—he wasn't sure which way to turn.

When his car and brain were both in gear again, he turned left for the hospital to pick up the little girl—the little stranger—who was his daughter. None of it seemed real.

He entered the hospital emergency room where he'd been told Elizabeth would be waiting and asked at the desk. "I'm looking for a child. Elizabeth Walters."

It still didn't seem real. The hospital smells with which he was so familiar assaulted his senses, yet the people around him blurred into the background. The woman at the desk had directed him to a room where a patient advocate was taking care of *his* child until *her father* arrived.

The first thing that caught his eye was her curly red hair. Andy had seen her briefly when he went to Susan's, but her mother had whisked her off to her bedroom in a hurry. At the time, Susan hadn't seemed to want him too close to Elizabeth, yet here he was, looking at the child he'd been called upon to care for—for how long he had no idea—and wondering what to do next.

Elizabeth sat at a little table with several toys in front of her, but her hands were empty. Andy saw her tear-stained face as she sat hugging herself and sniffling. The woman next to her was holding a teddy-bear she had offered to try to console her. Noticing the movement at the door the advocate looked up and smiled. Andy saw the relief on her face. She had obviously not been at ease trying to comfort the little one.

"Oh look, sweetie, your Daddy's here."

Elizabeth whipped around and Andy saw her face go from excited anticipation to disappointment and anger in an instant. "That's not my daddy!" She started to cry. "I want my momma." She wailed, "Where is she? I want my momma!"

"I'm sorry," the woman said to Andy. "I was told her father was coming, and I assumed it was you."

"It is," Andy said, "I mean I am… her father." The suspicious look told him to go on, so he motioned her aside and spoke quietly. "I mean I'm Dr. Reed. I'm, uh… I'm her biological father, but I didn't raise her." Andy saw something else on the woman's face then—perhaps judgment? —before she masked her visible emotions.

Elizabeth had moved behind the lady with the blue smock and was peeking out from around her. *How am I supposed to explain this to a five year old?* Nothing in all of his years as a psychologist had prepared him for this moment. He needed time to figure it all out. But there was no time. His shirt was soaked with perspiration. "It's awfully hot in here, I mean, I'm sorry… I'm not sure where we go from here."

Smock lady asked to see Andy's identification then explained she had only been asked to stay with the child until he arrived.

It was then that the arresting officer from the scene walked into the room. "Ma'am, would you mind staying with Elizabeth for a few more minutes while I talk with Dr. Reed?" He smiled at Elizabeth, who appeared calmer upon seeing him again. Once out in the hall the officer looked at Andy, tilted his head, and asked about his relationship with Susan Walters.

Through extreme embarrassment, Andy explained there had been a brief affair years earlier, but he had never been told he was Elizabeth's father until quite recently. "I'm afraid she doesn't know me at all, and I'm not sure exactly why I was called."

"Well, Ms. Walters said her husband wasn't around and gave us your name to call when she found out she wouldn't be going home tonight. We needed someone to care for the child." The officer explained that Susan had been intoxicated and ran her car into a tree. "She's very lucky neither of them were seriously injured. She's getting checked out, might have a mild concussion, but the child wasn't hurt at all... just scared."

"Thank God!" Andy said. *She's my little girl, but how do I make her understand?* "I'm a little worried though, Officer Miller. Do you think Elizabeth will be too afraid to go with me? I'm a stranger to her really."

"Tell you what. Ms. Walters hasn't been transported yet—she's still here—and she's sobered up a bit." The officer tilted his head and asked, "Do you think it would help if we take the child to see her, and maybe she can put her at ease? I mean, she did say to call you and all."

Andy had mixed feelings but shrugged. "Yeah, that's probably a good idea."

Elizabeth rushed to her mother's side as soon as she saw her, and the tears flowed pitifully. Andy watched as her mother tried to comfort and reassure her.

"It's going to be okay, sweetie," Susan murmured. "Dr. Reed is a very nice man, and you're going to be fine." Susan looked over Elizabeth's head at Andy hopefully.

He nodded. *This isn't the same woman.* Five years earlier she had been gorgeous. He remembered the perfectly styled blonde hair that now had about two inches of dark roots. She appeared gaunt, with dark circles under bloodshot eyes, and so much older than he remembered. No, this was not the Susan Walters of his past. This woman was a woeful drunk.

CHAPTER FIFTEEN

Val paced nervously, pulling back the curtains every few minutes… watching for headlights. She had been both relieved and puzzled when she got Andy's text.

SORRY, POLICE CALLED. SUSAN WAS IN AN ACCIDENT WITH ELIZABETH. BOTH OKAY. WILL EXPLAIN WHEN I GET HOME. LOVE YOU

Why would they call Andy? she wondered. *And where did he go?*

She checked the time. It was after midnight. "Where are you, Andy?"

She pulled the curtain back again just as his car turned into the driveway. Moments later, as he came through the kitchen, she heard him talking softly. *Is he on the phone this late?* Her question was answered when he came into sight with a little girl holding his hand.

Val's jaw dropped. *Oh my God! What's going on?* She closed her mouth and looking from him to the child and back, could think of nothing to say. At least nothing she could say out loud in front of a little girl.

Andy returned her look with an unspoken apology on his face. "Elizabeth, this is Mrs. Reed." He smiled sheepishly at Val. "This is Elizabeth."

Still stunned, Val gave her a half-smile, and said hello.

"Elizabeth's momma asked if she could stay with us tonight, and I said 'sure, we'll take good care of her for you'."

Val nodded then, with some effort, and gave the child her warmest smile. "Of course we will. You look tired, Elizabeth. Why don't we go up to the bedroom where my granddaughters stay when they come to visit?" She didn't think the five year old was going to respond, but when Andy ruffled her hair, she looked up at him and nodded her consent. When they got to the bedroom, Val turned to face her husband. "Andy, Elizabeth and I will be fine. Why don't you say goodnight now, and I'll find her some jammies to wear?" She smiled down at the little one and the frightened look on the child's face pulled at her heart.

It dawned on her now—Elizabeth hadn't spoken a word since they'd arrived. Andy said goodnight, and still not a word.

"So, does everyone always call you Elizabeth, or do they call you Lizzie… or Betsy?"

"My name's Elizabeth!" she pouted.

Val was satisfied that at least she could speak. "Well then, Elizabeth it is. Now these pajamas will be a little big for you—they belong to my granddaughters who are older—but they'll keep you nice and warm."

"How old are they?" she asked softly.

"What? Oh? Well, Mia is ten and Julie is eleven." She saw Elizabeth's jaw drop and realized how big an age difference it was. Susan's little girl reminded her of when Mia had been that age… when her mother Jenny had been killed by a drunk driver.

She swallowed the lump in her throat and found the smallest pair of pajamas she could. She held them up and they still looked huge. Glancing over her shoulder at the sad little face looking back she thought, *I've got to do better than this.* Then she had an idea. There was a pretty little teal nightshirt that might do the trick.

"Here we go. Let's try this, Elizabeth." It fit the five year old more like a long nightgown, but it worked. By the time she had her changed and pulled back the bedding, Val could see the poor child was exhausted. Her eyes were heavy and she was literally swaying. She allowed Val to lift her onto the bed and pull the covers up, and within seconds her eyes closed and she was breathing evenly.

Val turned on the nightlight, turned off the lamp, and tiptoed out of the room. She found Andy sitting on the side of the bed with his head in his hands. He looked up when she whispered his name.

"I'm so sorry. I didn't know what else to do," he said.

Val saw the distress etched into his brow, and felt sorry for him, but she had questions. She needed answers. She sat down next to him and took his hand in hers. "What happened, Andy? Why in the world is Susan's child sleeping in the other room right now?" As soon as the words 'Susan's child' were out of her mouth, she remembered this was also Andy's child. The reality was like a knife in her heart.

Andy looked up sharply. She knew he must be thinking the same thing.

He took a deep breath, then told her, as briefly as he could, about the accident and Susan's condition when it happened. "They said she never should have been driving. Not only was she intoxicated, but she lost her license the last time she had been stopped for driving under the influence. She could have been killed. *Elizabeth* could have been killed." His breath caught. "I don't know what the hell has happened to her, but she's messed up… and it's not the child's fault. Val, I couldn't just leave her there for them to call Children's Services." His eyes pleaded for understanding.

"Of course you couldn't," Val said after a short pause. "It's all right. We'll figure it out in the morning." She placed her hand on his cheek and added, with the first sign of a smile since she'd entered the bedroom, "You need to get some rest. You look like hell."

Val awoke to the sound of crying. Confused at first, she checked the bedside clock. It was three in the morning. She sat straight up with the sudden realization… it was Elizabeth. With a glance over her shoulder she saw Andy hadn't heard a thing. She jumped up and rushed to the child's bedside.

"It's okay, Elizabeth, it's okay."

The girl pulled away, eyes open wide but without recognition. She stared in fright and cried harder.

"Sweetie, it's okay. You're safe."

"Momma…" she cried looking around at unfamiliar surroundings. "Where's my momma?"

Val feared she was nearing hysteria.

"Hey, Elizabeth," Andy had awakened after all and was right behind her. He moved closer. "Remember me, sweetheart? It's Dr. Reed. Your momma asked me to take care of you tonight."

Val backed away in astonishment as Andy took the child in his arms. She clung to him, sobbing. He rocked her and said all the right things to comfort her until Elizabeth fell back to sleep.

"Thank you," she said to Andy when he joined her in the hall. "I tried to comfort her but couldn't. Yet she really responded to you," she added wondering if somehow, the child felt the bond of a father.

As though he understood her thoughts, Andy reminded her he was a psychologist. "She was only reassured because Susan told her she'd be okay with me… not because I'm her father."

"Yes, so you are," Val murmured as she turned toward their bedroom.

CHAPTER SIXTEEN

Susan sat in the drab, gray room where prisoners wait to see their visitors, but she wasn't sure he'd come. She hadn't talked to Marty in months, and the last time hadn't been pretty. That's why she was surprised when he actually showed up.

She tried to read the look on his face. Was it contempt or pity… or both? He shook his head. Perhaps it was just sadness she saw there. A terrible sadness. The kind that empties you. The kind she had felt every minute of every day since the accident.

"What happened to you, Susan?" he said.

"I don't know, I mean… I'm so sorry." She'd meant to speak, but all that came out was a whisper. Susan looked at her husband then looked away, too ashamed to maintain eye contact. "I hadn't really had that much to drink. I mean I was okay to drive. It was just the guy coming the other way had his bright lights on." She talked faster and faster and louder and louder like maybe if she said it loud enough and fast enough it would be true.

Marty shook his head. "Susan, I don't know what to say. You've got a problem."

Susan started to protest, but he cut her off.

"No Susan, you were drunk!"

She heard the anger in his voice.

"They showed me the report. I saw your blood alcohol level."

"But, you don't understand, Marty. I—"

"No! I'm not gonna listen to your excuses. You had Elizabeth in the car, for God's sake!" he said between clenched teeth. "She could have been killed… you both could have been killed." He stood up abruptly, turning his back on the woman he'd loved, married, and thought he had a child with. "I'm filing for divorce," he said with quiet determination.

She wasn't sure she heard him right. Months earlier, she had thought she wanted a divorce, but that was before. And she knew that's not what she really wanted. She had just wanted him to get off her back about the drinking, and then he'd threatened to take Elizabeth. She couldn't let that happen. He couldn't take her baby.

But she never meant to blurt out the truth. She had spoken out of fear. And now the fear was turning into panic.

"Marty, please, can't we talk? *Please*?"

"No, Susan. Not now. Not here, in this place." He looked at her, and she saw the pity in his eyes… and she hated it.

"Damn it, Marty! Listen to me. Damn you!" She cried and yelled at his back as he walked out the door… watched it shut behind him… closing the door on her last shred of hope.

♥

This was the time of day Susan hated most of all… lying there after lights out. She could shut it all out the rest of the day. From breakfast to lunch she kept busy working in the kitchen—whether she wanted to or not—then after lunch more work, then recreation time until dinner. Oh, and then there was her Alcoholics Anonymous group in the evening. She pretty much hated that too and knew she wasn't an alcoholic. Not like those other women. But as much as she hated that, this was worse.

Lying there in bed, she was cold, the kind of cold no number of blankets could cure. There was no escape. No escape from the bone chilling cold. No escape from her cell. No escape from her thoughts and memories.

She remembered the good times. She remembered bringing her beautiful baby home from the hospital and watching her sleeping peacefully in her bassinet. Holding her while she slept against her breast. Cheering as she took her first steps. Putting her on the bus for her first day of preschool. Susan Walters remembered all of it… every night.

Then she'd remember the bad times. Being late to meet her at the bus stop. Forgetting to give her lunch or dinner. Putting her in the back of the car when she ran out of vodka. *I just wanted to get something to drink. I wasn't really drunk.* She tossed and turned, unable to sleep. *I never meant to hurt you, Elizabeth.*

Susan was filled with self-loathing. She knew she'd had everything, and she threw it all away. She'd had a husband who loved her. She had a beautiful home. She had the most important thing of all, her little girl... and she still threw it away. And all she could think about was how much she wanted a drink. She missed the taste, the feel, the burn of her scotch... or wine... or vodka.

Of course, that was her secret. She attended her Alcoholics Anonymous meetings, and went through the motions. *I have to show them I've changed.* Susan was determined to get parole as soon as she was eligible. *I have to get out of here and back to Elizabeth.* She longed for the day she could hold her little girl and tuck her into bed. And she longed for a drink.

Susan lay awake listening to the occasional cough coming from one of the other cells. At two o'clock in the morning it was usually pretty quiet. All attempts at conversation had ended for the night, and all those able to sleep were creating a cacophony of diverse snoring and snorting noises. There were a couple of women whose snoring was even more obnoxious than Marty's had been.

But that's not what kept her awake. The closer it came to when she might get out of here, the more restless Susan became. She simply couldn't turn her brain off. She rehearsed every imaginable scenario until she thought she would go mad.

Sometime after two, she finally drifted into a restless sleep where she met up with her nightly demons. The dream started out in a room with five people staring at her from their chairs high on a platform.

Seated far below them she had to strain her neck to see their faces. They were all shouting questions at her. Susan wanted to answer them. She knew it was important. But she couldn't understand them. It all sounded like gibberish, so she started to scream back at them. "Stop it! Stop it! I can't understand you!" But the voices were deafening. They kept yelling at her to answer their questions. Then she was running. Unsure how she escaped the tiny room with the big chairs, she knew she was in trouble. She had to keep running. Something was after her... she had to keep running.

Then she found herself sitting in a dark room... hiding. But she wasn't alone—not completely alone—there was an old friend with her, and she was holding it tight. She took the top off the bottle of scotch and the smell was like home. About to take a drink—she could almost taste it—then the bottle vanished.

Daylight suddenly surrounded her. There was a bitter wind blowing. She was cold, so cold, but she didn't have a coat. She pulled the brown sweater tighter and looked around. She didn't recognize her surroundings, but it was a barren, wide-open space and there was no one around.

"Hello? Hello? Is anybody there?" She could feel someone's presence and strained to see who it was. Then she saw a figure in the distance. A tiny figure at the far end of a bridge. It was a child. "Elizabeth?" she whispered. Then louder, "Elizabeth!" Then she was running and screaming Elizabeth's name over and over.

No matter how far she ran, the distance between them never closed. The bridge grew longer. She fell to her knees, her face in her hands, and cried. When she looked up again, Elizabeth was standing right in front of her no more than ten feet away. The child had been crying as well, but was now looking at her mother, staring at her. Susan leapt to her feet to run to her child and instead ran straight into iron bars. Elizabeth turned and was walking away dragging her blanket behind her. The bridge crumbled behind her leaving an ever-growing impassable chasm.

Susan screamed and screamed... but without sound. No matter how hard she tried to scream to her daughter, nothing came out.

Susan sat straight up in bed. She was soaked with perspiration. She listened. Nothing had changed. *I must not have screamed out. No one is yelling.*

This wasn't the first time Susan had had that dream. It haunted her night after night. Sometimes there were subtle differences, but it always ended the same.

I've got to get out of here, or I'll lose my mind... Oh my sweet Elizabeth, I miss you so much. Susan got up and began pacing around her small space. After a few minutes, she sat back down on the side of her bed. *God, I need a drink!*

CHAPTER SEVENTEEN

Being a foster mother was exhausting. Val had forgotten what it was like to be with a five year old. It had been years since she'd spent time with children that age, and even then, it was only for an afternoon, or at the most, a weekend. But this was All. The. Time. *And I'm not getting any younger.*

She looked at the clock on the stove for the fifth time in twenty minutes and decided she'd better get to the bus stop. Elizabeth had been through enough lately. *Better early than risk being even a minute late.*

Andy had suggested they continue to let the school bus driver drop Elizabeth at the stop she was used to. It was less than a ten-minute drive from their house, and Val said she didn't mind. But it was one more thing. One more change in Val's life that she hadn't expected. Hadn't asked for… and didn't deserve.

She arrived in plenty of time and was checking messages on her phone when the bus pulled up. She watched as Elizabeth got off— looking so tiny climbing down the big steps—then looked toward her house and back at Val. Suddenly Val wasn't so sure it was a good idea for the child to see her house every day and not be able to go there.

Val remembered how much the little girl had cried when they went to get some of her clothes and toys. Once inside the house, she hadn't wanted to leave. Andy had needed to peel her off the bed, while she clung to the blanket dragging it with her.

Remembering the child's grief, Val was consumed with guilt for the resentment she'd felt just moments before. "Hi, Betsy!" she called.

For some reason, the child had decided after a few days that she wanted her foster parents to call her Betsy. Actually, it started as Beth but quickly morphed. Andy speculated it may be a way to distance or separate them from her real parents. From the time Elizabeth was a baby, Susan had refused to give her a nickname. No one had ever called her

Beth or Betsy. It was always Elizabeth with one exception... Marty called her Lizzie. And now she was adamant about no one but her daddy calling her that.

Betsy climbed into her booster seat in the back of the car, and Val leaned across to fasten her seatbelt wishing she had a vehicle that was more child friendly, but her days of driving a van had ended years ago. None of the grandchildren needed booster seats anymore.

Back in the driver's seat, Val glanced in the rearview mirror and saw a crease between the child's tiny brows. Betsy was *not* in a very good mood. "How was school today?" Val asked a little too brightly.

Hearing no answer, she put the car into gear and pulled away from the curb. Elizabeth stared out the window, and Val decided it was best to let her be until they got home.

"Okay, sweetie," Val said after parking in the garage, "we're home." She went around to the passenger's side and opened the back door to help the child out. That's when she realized her mistake.

Elizabeth had started to cry. "I want to go home," she sobbed.

She looked so miserable it broke Val's heart. "Oh honey, I know..." When Val lifted her out of the booster seat, she was surprised to find two little arms wrapped around her neck. She carried the child into the house with the red curls tickling her ear. Elizabeth held tight, weeping softly. When Val tried to put her down, Betsy clung tight. So, Val lowered herself into the big rocking recliner, child in tow, and the two rocked for a while. Within moments, Val heard the little one's even breathing and realized she had cried herself to sleep.

"Oh darlin', you poor thing." *It's just not fair. You don't deserve this.*

Andy found them still sitting there when he got home half an hour later.

Val hadn't heard him come in, but opened her eyes when she felt his presence. He was smiling as he watched her holding his daughter, but she saw the sadness behind his smile. "Andy, what are we going to do?" she asked in a whisper.

"What do you mean?"

"I mean, I'm falling in love with this little girl. What's going to happen?"

Before he could answer, Betsy stirred and rubbed her eyes. When she lifted her head and looked around, Val brushed her damp, sweaty hair back off of her face.

"Hey sleepyhead," Val spoke in a soothing voice, "they must have really worn you out at school today." Are you hungry? How about a little snack to hold you over 'til I can get supper ready?"

Betsy nodded and slid down from Val's lap.

"I'll get it," Andy offered. "What do we have in the kitchen? Let's go check, okay?" He took his daughter's hand and headed out of the room.

"There's some of the yogurt she likes in the fridge," Val called after them.

She stood and stretched wondering what to fix for dinner. It was getting kind of late to prepare the casserole she had planned, but she didn't regret spending the time holding Andy's little girl. They usually tried to eat healthy, and did fairly well, though this was beginning to feel like a carry-out night. But first she needed to freshen up.

A quarter of an hour later, as Val came down from the bedroom she heard laughter. She followed the sound to the family room where she found Andy and Betsy playing school. Betsy, of course, was the teacher, and her student was making silly mistakes in the rhyming game. Val joined in the laughter then ran to get her phone and started snapping pictures.

She took one especially good one of Betsy. Maybe she'd send it to Susan. *Maybe.*

"Okay, guys," Val raised her voice to be heard over the laughter. "I have a very important decision to make, and I need your help." The teacher and her student looked puzzled. "Well, it's getting to be dinner time. I'm hungry, and if I put a casserole in the oven, we may all starve before it's ready!" Val said dramatically. "So, all in favor of ordering a bacon pizza…"

"Yay!" the other two yelled in unison.

Pizza was always a hit, and if there was bacon involved, all the better. Twenty minutes later they were opening the pizza box. Val poured a glass of milk, and when she turned to put it in front of Betsy, the child had already bitten into the hot pizza and the cheese burned her lip. Spitting it out she looked up, eyes wide with fear.

"I'm sorry!" Betsy cried.

"It's okay, kiddo. It's too hot, ouch! Here…" Andy had grabbed a paper towel, wet it, and was holding it on the spot where the hot melted cheese had landed. "We just have to give it a few minutes to cool off."

"It smells so good it's hard to wait, isn't it?" Val soothed.

Of course it didn't take long before Betsy tried again, and as soon as it was cool enough, she really dug in. It wasn't the first time Andy and Val had watched with some dismay as the child stuffed food into her face as though she might not ever get to eat again.

"Why do you think she eats like that, Andy?" Val asked later as they lay in the dark.

Elizabeth had eaten more pizza than Val, and faster than either of them. She shoved so much into her mouth that her cheeks puffed out like a chipmunk.

"I'm afraid Betsy shows signs of having been seriously deprived."

"You mean Susan didn't feed her?" Val couldn't believe Susan Walters would starve her child.

"Afraid so. I doubt if she meant to, but I think once Marty left, her drinking got out of hand. The alcohol probably blinded her to the fact the child in front of her was starving."

CHAPTER EIGHTEEN

"Okay kids, remember, once they get here the dining room is off limits." Sarah wasn't usually nervous when her bridge group met at their house, but this would be the first time all four children were at home.

"Can't we even say hi to Grandma and everybody?" Mia was especially close to Val.

"Of course, you can take a few minutes to greet everyone and visit a little… *but* once we go in to play cards, you all have to disappear. Understood?"

"Yes, ma'am," came a chorus of four voices.

"Don't worry, angel, I'll keep all the ponies in the corral."

Craig's words were reassuring, and besides, she wondered why she was so nervous about it. There was no one in this group who would complain even if the kids did intrude.

"Thanks, hon. What are you guys going to do while we're playing?"

"Cody, the girls, and I are going to play a game—I think they settled on Life—and Bobby said he's just going to watch and maybe work on his model." There was a knock on the front door, and they heard it open. "Must be Mom." Craig went to greet Val, but nearly got trampled by his four hooligans.

Sarah stood back and smiled. It never ceased to amaze her how excited the kids still got every time they saw their grandmother. When Val finally managed to make her way through the troop of children into the kitchen, Sarah thought she looked tired.

"Hi there," Val said, giving her a warm hug.

"How are things going with your little foster child?"

Sarah couldn't quite understand why her in-laws would take on such a burden at their age, but she knew they had big hearts and Christian spirits. Still, she worried. So did Craig. She saw the slight hesitation before Val smiled and told her how attached she was becoming to Betsy.

"Well, don't get too attached," Sarah warned.

They were interrupted as the commotion of the latest arrivals moved their way. "Aunt Bonnie and Miss Kathy are here," Bobby shouted.

"Yes, I can see that. Okay, settle down, guys," Sarah cautioned.

"Yep, you guys heard the boss," Craig said, steering his little crowd toward the family room. "We got our marching orders... we are banished. Have fun, ladies."

It didn't take long for the bridge foursome to load their plates with cheese, veggies and dip, and of course a few cookies. They gathered round the dining room table which was the perfect size with the leaves removed.

Sarah had munched enough veggies before her guests arrived and sunk her teeth into one of the still slightly warm snickerdoodles. "Mmm, these are so good. Thanks for giving me your recipe, Val." She'd had a hard time not chomping into them as soon as they were ready. That hot-out-of-the-oven smell had proved too tempting for Craig and the kids who had each had just one before she shooed them away with the promise of a plateful in the family room later just for them.

Val laughed, "How did you manage to save us any? The kids love these, especially the biggest kid, Craig."

Sarah noticed how her mother-in-law's face morphed when she talked about her son and grandchildren. Much of the strain she'd seen earlier melted away.

The fun continued in between some totally serious bidding and playing of the hands. Bonnie and Val won the first rubber, but Sarah's slick play helped her and Kathy squeak out a win by the end of the night.

"Way to go, partner!" Kathy said when Sarah pulled in the final trick. Since she had been such a novice when she joined the group, it thrilled her to win. Especially when she knew she hadn't screwed up.

Bonnie was the first to push away from the table and pick up her plate to take to the kitchen. "Well, it's been fun, ladies—always is—but I think I'm going to head on home. Frank always waits up for me, and he's been looking kind of tired the last couple days. I think we'll make it an early night."

Sarah had noticed that Bonnie didn't seem completely herself all evening. She thought her former professor had seemed distracted but didn't want to think that was why she'd won.

"I'll walk out with you," Kathy chimed in. "I've also got someone waiting for me. I'm not really tired, but we'll probably head to bed early—and not to sleep, if you get my drift." Everyone clearly got her drift since Kathy and her husband were still practically newlyweds.

"Well now," Bonnie said over her shoulder, "I didn't say Frank and I were necessarily going to sleep, did I?"

Sarah heard Kathy scolding her as they headed out into the chilly night and turned to Val. "That Bonnie is such a stitch. I just love her. And I know you do. My gosh, how long have you two been friends, anyway?"

"A long time, Sarah. I met Bonnie when I married Andy, and we just clicked." Val headed to the family room to go say goodnight to her son. "Are the kids in bed already?" she asked looking at her watch. "Oh yeah, ten o'clock on a school night. Of course they are." She sighed, "Well, I guess I'd better get home myself. I'm anxious to see how your dad made out with Betsy tonight."

"Why, is there a problem?" Sarah asked.

"Oh, no, not really. Betsy can just be a little moody. But Andy's really good with her," she laughed. "His skills as a therapist are paying off."

♥

"Alone at last." Craig pulled Sarah down on his lap.

She giggled in protest saying she needed to finish putting the dishes in the dishwasher.

"They'll be there in the morning," he murmured kissing her neck.

"Mmm, that's very tempting, but you know I might not feel up to cleaning the kitchen in the morning… that's not my best time of day."

"I'll take care of it. Now stop talking about dishes. As a matter of fact, just stop talking."

Before she could respond, his mouth was on hers so she couldn't utter a word. The only sound she could make was a hum of contentment.

CHAPTER NINETEEN

Val had been filled with self-pity because her life was turned upside down. Now she realized her life wasn't so bad at all.

Death puts life in perspective.

She looked through the crowd of people surrounding Bonnie and thanked God for her husband. Andy stood by her side, his right hand on her back, and looked straight ahead. His face was taut with the strain of not crying. He wouldn't cry. Not here. Not now.

Frank had been one of his best friends. He loved their golf games and hanging out together in the nineteenth hole afterwards. Now their usual Saturday morning foursome would be missing their old-timer. Val knew her husband was hurting, but he would hold up in front of others. *I hope I can do the same.* Val knew she needed to be strong for her friend although Bonnie looked quite courageous standing there accepting everyone's condolences.

Frank had been loved by so many people, and they all seemed to have come for the viewing before the service. "I think our entire church membership must be here," she whispered to Andy, "and all the staff from the university."

"Yeah, the parking lot is full now, and they're parking across the street on the Baptist church lot."

Bonnie didn't know how many times she had said thank you as people, one after another, said how sorry they were. *'If there's anything I can do...' 'I'm here for you...' 'We know he's in a better place...' 'Call me anytime...'* She knew they all meant it. These were her friends, and she felt their love and sympathy, but now she was bone weary. She was just so tired of saying thank you, of having to be present, to be strong.

She felt a hand on her shoulder and knew before looking it was her son, Mark. She looked up into his eyes. *I never realized, he has Frank's eyes.*

"How are you doing, Mom? Maybe you should come sit down for a while. You look exhausted."

"Okay, yes, maybe for a few minutes… but only a moment's rest." She let Mark lead her into a room where she could sit quietly before the service. She didn't cry. There were no tears left. Sinking into the chair next to her son, Bonnie looked at him and shored herself up. *Come on, the children need you.*

"Mom, Dana and I have been talking, and I want you to know we'll stay through the weekend, and then, if you want, you can come stay with us for a while. We have that spare room, and you know the kids would love to have you there."

Bonnie reached over and patted his hand. "Thank you, Mark. I appreciate that. I really do. Beth made me the same offer, but I don't think so. At least not yet." She looked down at the floor.

Mark said something else, but she didn't hear him. She was hearing Frank's voice. She remembered a conversation they'd had two days ago.

It was a Thursday night after her ladies' bridge group finished and all the others went home. Frank had been reading in the study as was his habit when the game was at their house. After cleaning up, she went to the study expecting to find him asleep with the book in his lap. That was how she found him more often than not. But he wasn't asleep. And he wasn't reading.

"Well you look quite pensive, dear. What are you thinking about?" That's when she saw the papers in his hands. "What are you looking at?"

"I was just going over our wills." He looked up and gave her a half-smile. "I think we've covered everything pretty well, but…"

"But what?" Bonnie felt gooseflesh on her arms. She wasn't sure why, but she was uneasy.

"Well, we never talked specifically about funeral arrangements." Bonnie dropped into her rocking chair, the one she'd sat in by her

husband's side for so many years. She groped for words, but her mouth was dry.

"We covered the most important things," Frank went on to say, "but not some of the details like what music we'd like." Bonnie opened her mouth to speak but hesitated. Before she could form the question on her mind, Frank continued, "I've jotted down a few notes. Nothing major… just like," he smiled into her eyes, "I'd like to have The Old Rugged Cross."

"Of course," Bonnie said, "but why are you telling me this now?" Her voice quivered. "Are you feeling okay? Are you having chest pains?" She was already reaching for her phone when he reassured her he was fine.

But were you really, Frank? Were you really?

"Mom, are you okay?" It was her daughter, Laura, and Bonnie realized she had no idea what Laura had said.

"Yes, hon, I'm okay." Then she laughed a little. "Well as okay as can be expected."

♥

The funeral had been exactly what Frank wanted, and now all the family and close friends were gathered at the house. People were telling stories, sharing memories, sometimes laughing, sometimes crying, and Bonnie watched it all from a place far away. She was there physically, of course. She accepted their hugs, talked, and laughed at the grandchildren who were finally a little less subdued. She was glad to see them being more themselves. With them all living so far away, her opportunities to spend time with them were limited.

They were supposed to come for Christmas, but not this soon. Bonnie remembered sitting at the Thanksgiving table with the Reeds and all their grandchildren and the newest addition to their family, and thinking she couldn't wait to see her own grandchildren. She told Val she could hardly wait. Now here they were.

Bonnie excused herself and went into the bathroom, the only place she could possibly be alone with all these people in the house. There were more tears after all.

When she managed to stop the flow, she braced herself and ventured back into the throng of people milling about. She spied Val standing by a window staring out into the dying day and knew the one person she wanted to be with at this moment.

"How about a cup of tea, my friend?"

Val jumped at the sound of Bonnie's voice in her ear. "That would be lovely, Bonnie. Lead the way."

There were several people in the kitchen talking, so the ladies took their teacups into the study.

"Oh, there you are, Mom. Can I get you anything?" It was Bonnie's middle daughter, Beth, who had escaped to the study with her husband Adam. "We have to go check on the kids, but if you need anything…"

"No, Beth, we're fine. Val and I have a few things we need to discuss if you don't mind."

Once alone, Bonnie collapsed into her usual rocking chair and Val sat on the loveseat. They both looked at Frank's chair, and as her eyes welled up, Bonnie didn't have to hide it. She quickly dabbed with a tissue grabbed from the box on the table.

"That will be the hardest part, you know… him not being in that chair… not being at the dinner table. Not being in our bed." Bonnie's voice cracked and her breath caught.

Val bit her lower lip. "I'm so sorry. I wish there was something I could say or do that would help, but I know there isn't."

"You see, that's why you're the one person I needed to be with right now. You understand. Everyone else keeps trying to say something that will help, but they can't." Bonnie folded her hands in her lap. "Only God can help me, really. No, I'm sorry. I don't mean that." She smiled at her friend. "It does help that you're here for me. Some of the others, too. The love and support of the children and my dear friends does help."

"I'm here, Bonnie. And I'll keep being here… no more than a phone call away."

"I know, dear, and I appreciate it more than I can say. But you have the child to take care of now. How is she, by the way?"

"Well, she doesn't cry nearly as much as she did at first, but it's rough. She still misses her mother."

"Of course she does." Bonnie understood missing someone you love as she glanced again at Frank's empty chair.

CHAPTER TWENTY

Val helped Betsy get on the school bus then rushed back to the warmth of her car and headed for Bonnie's. She wasn't sure how her friend was going to get through the holiday this year, but if there was any way to help, Val was determined to find it.

She pulled into Bonnie's driveway and saw her coming out the door. She must have been watching from the window. "Good morning," Bonnie greeted her cheerily as she hopped in the car.

"Are you hungry?" Val asked.

"Yes, I think I'm getting my appetite back." Bonnie had been forgetting to eat in the days following Frank's death, and said she found it difficult to eat alone in her empty house. "I'm ready for a nice unhealthy stack of hotcakes. Can we go to IHOP?"

"Sounds good to me. I think I'll go for broke and get mine with strawberries and whipped cream."

Val parked a short distance from the entrance and jumped out. She noticed Bonnie was still sitting in the passenger seat, so she walked around to the other side of the car.

Bonnie glanced out the window at her with sudden recognition. She opened the door and laughed, "Oh my, I'm losing my mind. I was waiting for Frank to come around and open my door."

They hurried in out of the cold, and when the hostess led them to a booth, Val thought Bonnie looked relieved. "Are you okay, Bonnie?"

"Oh… yes, I know it's silly, but I was just worried she would put us where Frank and I usually sat. You know we used to come here on Saturday mornings, and we usually settled over there." She pointed in the direction of a booth where a young couple was seated.

"I don't think you're being silly at all. I can't imagine how hard it must be for you to be here without him. Maybe we should have gone somewhere else."

"Now you're being silly." Bonnie grinned. "Frank and I have been to most of the restaurants in this town. If I don't go anywhere the two of us went… well, I guess I won't be going out much." She winked and opened the menu then closed it almost immediately. "I don't know why I'm looking at this. I know what I want."

The two friends talked about Betsy and Val's grandchildren until their food came, and it wasn't until they had polished off their short stacks that Bonnie became more serious.

"You know, Val, I'm thinking about selling the house."

Val's jaw dropped. "Oh Bonnie, but your home is so beautiful! Oh… I'm sorry."

"No, don't be sorry. You're right. We brought so many things from our travels and decorated it over time to be perfect for us… and it was… perfect *for us,* that is. But now…" Bonnie picked up her tea and took a sip. "Now, it's too filled with memories. Not that I want to forget, mind you, but it's so hard." She had been staring down into her teacup. Now she leaned against the back of the booth and smiled up at her friend. "However, I know it isn't wise to make such a major life change so soon after—"

"No… that's right, Bonnie. Don't do anything yet."

"Don't worry, dear. I won't, but I feel like I need a little break from that house for a while. I haven't decided exactly what I'm going to do, but you're the best friend I have in this world, especially now that Frank is gone, and I had to let you know what I'm thinking." Bonnie stared at her wedding ring then looked skyward. "Maybe I'll go visit with one of the kids for a little while. All three of them invited me, though Laurie seemed a little less enthusiastic about it than Mark or Beth. Perhaps she's afraid I won't approve of her single lifestyle."

"I can't imagine she'd think that, Bonnie. You've got to be the most non-judgmental person I know."

"Well, I certainly try not to judge, but you know the relationship between a mother and daughter can be pretty complicated."

Not really. Val thought of the baby girl she'd lost at birth. Then she thought of the little girl she'd just put on the school bus. *But she's not mine.*

"Anyway, I don't think Laura really has enough room, and I get the impression she's not home a lot. It sounds like she works sixty-hour weeks, and then there's her social life. So, I was thinking about going out to spend some time with Mark. But even though I think I have a good relationship with Dana, I don't know how comfortable my daughter-in-law would be with me staying there for more than a couple of days." Bonne sighed and refilled her teacup. "Did you want more coffee, Val?"

"Yeah, I saw her bringing it around for refills." Val nodded toward their waitress.

"So, maybe I could stay with Beth and Adam. Matt is away at college now, so Beth said I could have his room, and they have such a big house I don't think we'd get in each other's way." Bonnie laughed, "Although I'm not sure what it will be like in a house with the other two boys. Imagine going from the quiet house of two old people to what's probably a pretty raucous environment with a ten and thirteen-year-old boy. Those two really get into it sometimes." Bonnie rolled her eyes as she described some of the tussles they'd gotten into on visits to her house. "And they were probably on their best behavior then!"

"Yeah," Val laughed, "I guess I had it easy with an only child. I never had to live with the arguing… except maybe with me," she laughed again, "when he was in those early teen years."

"I don't remember Craig ever being anything but polite," Bonnie said with raised eyebrows.

"Ah, well, he knew better than to act up in front of other people… plus he always respected you too much. He would have been afraid to disappoint you… but I was just 'Mom'." Val laughed at the memory. "Fortunately, that stage didn't last too long with Craig, though. You're right, Bonnie, he was a good kid."

"And grew up to be a wonderful man—husband and father—a man you can be proud of," Bonnie added. "So anyhow, I haven't made up my mind, but I feel like I have to do something soon."

"You know what?" Val tilted her head and squinted her eyes. "I have kind of a crazy idea. What would you think of not leaving town? What would you think of coming to stay with us for a while?"

Bonnie started to laugh, then her eyes widened. "Oh, you're serious?"

"Yes, I'm serious. Think about it. You'd be out of your house, removed from some of the painful memories, but not so far away that you couldn't check on things from time to time… and you know we have plenty of room."

"But what about Andy?"

"What about him? You know he wouldn't mind at all. As a matter of fact, I know he'd love to have you. Of course, there is a little five year old in the house, so it's not as quiet as it used to be, especially since she's started to relax more around us."

"But Val, you have your hands full with her… although, possibly I could help you with that."

Val could see the wheels turning.

"Would you let me maybe watch her sometimes," Bonnie suggested, "and give you a break?"

"Would I ever!" Val got excited about the idea of sharing the responsibility of caring for Betsy, at least for a little while. She looked at her friend expectantly.

"I'll tell you what," Bonnie crossed her arms and let a smile lift her lips, "how about if you discuss it with Andy, and let me sleep on it?"

"Fabulous!" Excited by the thought of her best friend staying with them, Val felt like a school girl getting ready for a sleepover with her bestie. *And I would have help with Betsy!*

CHAPTER TWENTY-ONE

Sarah sat smiling, legs tucked under her, sipping an eggnog and watching the scene before her.

"And it came to pass in those days, that there went out a decree from Caesar Augustus that all the world should be taxed…" Craig read. Mia sat to her father's left with Julie next to her, and Cody and Bobby were on their dad's other side. Craig always read the Christmas story from the St. James version of the Bible, just as Andy had read it to him.

The Christmas tree, covered with lights and special ornaments, dripped with icicles and bathed the room with the fresh scent of pine. *This is perfect,* Sarah thought. The children listened with rapt attention as though they were hearing the story for the very first time though this was a Christmas Eve tradition.

"…And she brought forth her firstborn son, and wrapped him in swaddling clothes, and laid him in a manger; because there was no room for them in the inn."

Sarah, of course, knew the story by heart and loved the tradition as much as her husband, but her mind wandered to another time. A time in the future. A time when there would be five children gathered around their father to listen and learn the true meaning of this special holiday.

Craig closed the Bible and looked into the eyes of each child. "Always remember, in the midst of all the commercialism, this is what it's really all about." Then his serious expression transitioned into a big grin. "Now, who wants a couple of Christmas cookies before you head into bed?" With a chorus of *me's,* and *I do's* the foursome sprinted to the kitchen nearly knocking each other down.

"Just two!" Sarah called after them, "and then you're off to bed. And don't take the ones from Santa's plate," she added following them to pour the milk.

Sarah plopped down on the couch next to her husband nearly an hour later. "I think they're all asleep *finally.*" She felt Craig's arm encircle her but knew it was too soon. "Hold on there, Bucky. We've still got those special things to put under the tree before we get too distracted," she warned.

"Aw, but I can't wait to give you an early present," Craig teased.

Sarah pushed him to arm's length. "You are so bad!" she said.

"Are you okay?" Craig asked after Sarah grew silent.

"Yes, I couldn't be better," she sighed, "I just wish everyone could be as blessed as we are. But not everyone is."

"Are you thinking of anyone in particular?"

"Yeah, actually I was thinking of the client I went in to see today." Sarah's work counseling victims of abuse usually didn't get to her—she had learned to compartmentalize—but tonight her thoughts went to that nineteen year old for whom this Christmas was not a joyous holiday. "I gave her my number just in case it got too bad tomorrow, but she has some pretty good support at the shelter." Sarah brightened, "I think she'll be all right, and I told her I'd see her the day after Christmas." Sarah always felt better after sharing her worries with her husband. "Now, let's get the rest of those presents under the tree, and I just might have a little gift for you before we go to sleep." She winked and bounded off the couch to make quick of the work ahead.

"So, what is this special gift you have for me?" Craig was looking around the bedroom for any signs of shiny wrapping paper.

Sarah slid under the covers and lifted the blanket for him to join her. "It's not a package, and it's not wrapped." Her smile hid a secret she couldn't bear to keep for one more minute. "And no, it's not that," she laughed as he reached for her. "After I saw that client today, I had another appointment." Craig's eyebrows shot up. "I saw my Ob/Gyn today. It's official."

This time she let Craig pull her close. After a warm embrace, he took her chin in his hand. "Are we crazy, angel?"

She nodded, "Probably… but it's a good kind of crazy."

They laughed and snuggled a while before Craig became quite serious. "Does this mean we can't try anymore?" he said in mock horror.

Between fits of giggles, Sarah assured him they could *pretend* they still needed to try. "I can't wait to see the kids' reaction to the news, but I'm not ready to share it just yet, okay?"

Craig agreed it would be better to wait a while. Until she got safely through the first trimester. "So, Mrs. Reed, if you'll recall, I said I had a present I want to give you."

Sarah felt the familiar tingle as their lips met. And later, as she was drifting off to sleep she thought, *Best Christmas gift ever...*

CHAPTER TWENTY-TWO

Christmas was different this year. Especially for Bonnie. But everyone went through the motions, and the children had a wonderful time. Well most of them anyway.

But one little girl had the saddest holiday of her short life. Christmas morning found many presents under the tree in the Reed household. There were presents for Bobby Jr., Julie, Codie, Mia, and Betsy. The older children had accepted Betsy more easily than Val and Andy expected, probably because they had all been through significant losses themselves. Val remembered the first Christmas after Jenny was killed by a drunk driver. Craig had been devastated. If it hadn't been for their children, Cody and Mia, Val wasn't sure he would have survived the loss, and he certainly wouldn't have celebrated Christmas.

However, he did have them, and those two children were his reason for living. He knew his Jenny would be disappointed if he didn't give them a good Christmas and a good life. Then Sarah came along. She went from being the nice girl who cut his hair, to his good friend and confidante, to his love, his wife, and the mother of their four children.

Sarah was familiar with grief, having lost her own husband, Bobby, to cancer two years earlier. It was a strange bond upon which they built their friendship and more. Each alone with children—but not from divorce. Somehow they created a blended family filled with love. Cody and Mia had pictures of their mother so they would never forget her. Julie and Bobby Jr. had pictures of their father, too.

And Val thanked God every day for the blessing of Craig and Sarah finding each other.

Whenever the young Reed family came to visit their grandparents or when Val and Andy went to their house, Craig and Sarah's children doted on the newcomer. Mia was very protective of Betsy, not knowing the girl was actually her aunt... her father's much, much younger sister.

Craig had been shocked when Andy finally told him everything. It was hard to hear about the affair—cheating on his mother—but he certainly didn't want to take it out on his new little sister. Forgiveness, however, would take time.

When Craig, Sarah, and the four children got to the house on Christmas day, Val hoped it would lift Betsy's spirits. They all brought her presents they had made for her, and her mood did improve for a while. She was especially happy with the gift from Mia who had written an acrostic poem for her name and drawn a lovely picture to go with it.

Be my friend
Every day and forever
Tell me your secrets
Share all your dreams
You are my special friend

Mia had some real talent for a ten year old, and art class was one of her favorites. Her teacher had helped her with an abstract watercolor painting filled with hearts. Then they had scanned it into the computer, put the poem on it in a beautiful font, and framed it. Val could see Mia's gift had more meaning for Betsy than all the other presents under the tree.

Betsy hugged Mia then hugged the picture to her chest. She looked at Val hopefully. "Can we hang it in my room?"

Val had tried to make it feel like "Betsy's room" and not just her granddaughters' room that Betsy now occupied, and this would add to that feeling.

"Of course, we can. Let's do it right now. Andy, you want to give us a hand?"

Mia watched proudly as Betsy chose the perfect spot to hang it, and Andy took down another picture and put hers in its place. He asked Betsy how it looked and she said she loved it. Mia smiled, then her grandpa came over and whispered to her, "Thank you, sweetie."

Val, who'd been watching the exchange, saw the puzzled expression on Mia's face. Though her granddaughter might not understand Andy's appreciation, Val knew it had everything to do with the big grin on Betsy's face. *But I wonder how long that smile will last.*

The answer came even sooner than she might have anticipated. Shortly after the picture was hung, the children were caught up in their own presents. Mia was busy with her new sketchpad and colored pencils, Cody and Bobby Jr. were working together constructing a Lego spaceship, and Julie was reading a new book—happiest when lost in one of her fantasies.

Val looked around at the peaceful scene, only half listening to the adult conversation. But someone was missing. Her eyes scanned the room. There was no sign of Betsy. She'd vanished without saying a word. Val quietly got to her feet to look around.

"Where are you going, dear?" Andy asked.

"I'll be right back." Val chose not to share her concerns until she was sure there was a reason.

She found Betsy lying on her bed, clutching her blanket and crying into her pillow.

Val considered leaving her alone—Betsy sometimes needed time— but reconsidered. Instead, she sat down on the side of the bed and stroked the child's hair. "What's wrong, sweetie?" Val knew it was a ridiculous question. She knew exactly what was wrong, but she asked anyway.

"I miss my momma," was the muffled reply that came from the pillow.

Val felt lost. She didn't know how to make it better. The one thing this little girl wanted for Christmas was the one thing Val couldn't give. She felt more than heard someone else in the room and turned to see Mia standing quietly in the doorway. The older child approached, and Val recognized something in her eyes. It took a moment before she realized why it was familiar. It was the sadness she had seen more than five years earlier when Mia had her first Christmas without Jenny.

Val moved aside as Mia came closer and, without a word to her grandma, climbed on the bed.

"Can I keep you company, Betsy?"

Val saw the little one nod her head, and Mia snuggled in putting her arm around the younger child.

Val moved to the door, looked back once, and seeing the two girls, knew Betsy's best medicine right now was Mia.

Chapter Twenty-Three

Bonnie stood in the cold wind, pulling her coat tightly around her, and wiped her nose with her gloved hand. It had turned colder overnight—bitterly cold—just in time for Christmas. The silver-white grass crunched beneath her feet as she shuffled from one to the other.

"This isn't the Christmas I'd planned, Frank. Why did you have to go and leave me so soon?" She hugged herself and felt totally alone. "I know we're not supposed to ask why, God, but it's so hard. We had such plans, didn't we, Frank? Now that we were both retired, we were going to travel back to Italy."

Frank's headstone blurred as tears filled her eyes and streamed down her face. She brushed them away with the back of her hand. *Stop it, Bonnie.*

"The kids are all back at the house. They wanted to spend Christmas in the family home one more time. They're not too happy with me right now. They don't think I should sell the place, but I can't stand it without you." She sobbed and put her hand on the stone to steady herself. "You understand, don't you, Frank?"

Bonnie felt a calm reassurance enfolding her and smiled through the tears.

"Thank you, Lord."

She took a few steps backward, then slowly turned. She only looked back once before reaching her car. She turned the engine on and sat quite still, glad to be out of the wind but not wanting to leave… not yet. She stared back toward the grave that held the other half of her heart then blew her nose.

The children and grandchildren would worry if she didn't get back soon. They hadn't wanted her to come to the cemetery alone, worrying it was too cold. Laura had been the worst, and Bonnie had finally snapped.

"I'm not so old and feeble that I can't take care of myself, and I'm certainly not a child. Please don't treat me like one."

"I'm sorry, Mom," Laura had stammered.

"No, no, I'm sorry." Bonnie embraced her daughter then pushed her to arm's length and looked into her eyes. "I shouldn't have snapped at you. But you have to understand, Laura, I need to do this, and I need to go by myself, okay?"

And so she had. Now, sitting alone in the car she breathed deeply and spoke to her husband once more.

"Oh Frank, I don't know how to be happy again. We'll get through the holidays all right. I know how to go through the motions for the children." A smile crossed her face. "The service was beautiful last night. You would have loved it, especially the Hallelujah Chorus. I had chills."

In that moment, she didn't feel so alone. Her body warmed and her cheeks flushed. "I know you're here with me, Frank. I can feel it… but I can't see you or touch your cheek." Tears slipped from the corners of her eyes, and she didn't bother wiping them away. "I can't stay in that house, you know. The memories hurt too much. Too many reminders."

The children had strongly objected to her selling the house, but they were coming around to the idea. They only visited a couple times a year and all three had admitted they kept expecting to see Dad walk into the room. It was so much worse for Bonnie. After praying about it, she knew it was the right decision for her.

"I need to let you go for a while, dear. God has called you home, but apparently, there's still more for me to do here… yet I know I'll see you again. And when I do, we'll never have to be apart."

Bonnie grabbed another tissue from the box sitting on the passenger seat and blew her nose. She was ready to go back to the madness now. As much as she loved her children and grandchildren, when they were all there at the same time, she found it a bit chaotic. A drastic change from the silence she'd walked with in the weeks following Frank's stroke. *I'm not sure which is worse.*

She put the car in gear and slowly pulled out of the cemetery and onto the country road that led back to town. Bonnie had always loved the drive through Chestnut Hill. The road was lined with beautiful, tall pine trees that made it feel magical. At intervals she could spy the luxurious homes nestled behind them. They were especially gorgeous now, tastefully adorned with Christmas lights. She drove slowly, stealing looks and wondering what was happening behind each wreath-embellished door.

She imagined happy families gathered 'round for the holiday, but were they all happy? Or did any of those homes conceal loneliness and depression? Was there another lonely widow missing the man she had always shared every holiday with? Or a lonely man longing to speak to his wife one more time?

Stop it, Bonnie!

She did her best to shake it off as she pulled into her garage and turned off the engine. As she opened the door into the mudroom, she heard the cacophony of five grandchildren having fun. Since her son, Mark, and her daughter, Beth, lived in separate states, the cousins rarely got together and totally took advantage of the opportunity to play games and enjoy their time together when they did. It was almost always at Grandma's house, and Bonnie thought it would be kind of sad not to have these gatherings. How could they do this if she downsized? For the first time, she began to have second thoughts about her decision to move.

CHAPTER TWENTY-FOUR

Holding them at arm's length, Val carried the still damp sheets to the laundry room and stuffed them into the washer. She started the cycle then took a deep breath in through her nose counting to five and blew it out slowly counting to eight. She hoped the discipline she practiced at yoga class would help her let go of the anger, but this was not how she had planned to spend her morning… and inhaling the smell of urine didn't have a calming effect. *Thanks for ruining my brunch plans, Betsy.*

After thoroughly spraying the laundry room with Febreze, Val headed back to the kitchen and grabbed her phone off the island.

"Hi, Bonnie. I'm afraid I'm not going to make it this morning after all."

"Sorry to hear that. Are you okay?"

"More or less. But I'm stuck doing extra laundry. Betsy wet the bed again last night. I'm glad I decided to get that mattress protector."

"Oh, is that all," Bonnie said, then quickly added, "You must be exhausted, but I'm glad you aren't ill."

Val realized her friend was letting her off the hook for making a mountain out of a mole hill, but she couldn't help feeling resentment. "This was the third time this week. It's getting old really quick, if you know what I mean."

"I'm sure it is. But listen, why don't we still get together? Could we squeeze in a late lunch?"

"Well," Val thought about the article waiting for her in her study and the deadlines she had to meet. "You know what, let's just do it. I'll get some work done on my reviews while I'm finishing the laundry. Then I can make up her bed and… how about one o'clock? That way we'll be done in time for me to still meet her at the bus."

The pile of papers on her desk beckoned, and Val was lost in work when the phone rang. She was going to ignore it, but didn't dare take the chance of missing an important call. She checked the caller ID and groaned. It was the school. Not the Madison Intermediate School Mia and Cody attended but the K-3 Elementary where Betsy was enrolled. *Now what?*

It was forty-five minutes later when Val pulled up the recent calls on her cell and dialed Bonnie back. Betsy was tucked into bed in the guest room. Val hoped there wouldn't be any accidents, since that bed did not have a mattress protector on it. The child only seemed to have her bed-wetting problems at night… so far.

"Hi Bonnie, guess what… I won't be able to meet you for lunch after all." Val didn't bother hiding the disgust in her tone.

Bonnie expressed her own disappointment and concern. "Has something else happened? Are you sure you're okay?" she asked.

Val explained the call from the school nurse. "So I had to go pick up Andy's daughter." The last two words caught in her throat, but that's how she thought of Betsy when she was especially tired and resentful.

"They said she complained of a bellyache and then she threw up again."

"Again?" Bonnie wasn't aware of this being a problem.

"Afraid so. The same thing happened last Friday. She's been complaining of tummy-aches a lot lately. I just made an appointment with the pediatrician Susan used, and I'm going to take Betsy in to be checked." Val flopped down on the couch in the family room and rubbed her head. She'd really been looking forward to spending a couple of hours with her best friend.

"I have an idea," Bonnie said. "How about if I bring the mountain to Mohammed? Let me bring lunch… or did you already eat something?"

"No, I actually haven't eaten anything." Val sat forward hopefully. "Are you sure you don't mind?"

"Wouldn't have suggested it unless I wanted to, my friend. Should I get something for Betsy, too?"

"Yes, maybe chicken noodle soup that she can try later." When she ended the call, Val looked in the guest room, and Betsy was either asleep or pretending to be, so she quietly closed the door and went to put the sheets in the dryer.

Normally she would already have made up her foster child's bed with different sheets... but the ones in the wash were Betsy's favorites. Probably because Mia had picked them out.

When Bonnie arrived, they decided to eat in the breakfast nook off the kitchen. Val brewed a chocolate mint tea—one of Bonnie's favorites—from the loose tea she'd come to prefer. With her friend's help, she had discovered it was vastly better than the bags. That was only one of many things she'd learned from Bonnie over their long years of friendship. Val brought the pot to the table and poured them each a cup while Bonnie took the soup and sandwiches out of their containers.

Sitting across from her friend, Val blew out her breath. She read the concern in her friend's eyes and hastened to assure her she was fine. Just tired.

"Are you sure?" Bonnie asked. "You haven't quite been yourself lately."

Val tried to deny it, but her voice cracked and her eyes began to well. With the back of her hand she swiped away the tears that escaped to run down her cheeks.

Bonnie jumped up and retrieved tissues, patted her shoulder, then waited quietly.

That's what Val loved about Bonnie. She had the patience of a saint.

Val blew her nose and sniffed a few times before she found her voice. "I'm sorry. I'm being ridiculous. Compared to what you've been going through, I don't have a problem in the world, and here I sit sobbing like a fool."

"You're not a fool, Val, and there's no sense comparing your pain to someone else's. You know that."

They'd had this discussion before. Bonnie had explained that knowing another person lost a leg doesn't make it hurt any less when you stub your own toe.

"Don't put yourself down, Val. Acknowledge what you're feeling."

She knew Bonnie was right, but the words stuck in her throat. Her friend blurred behind the tears as she broke through the barrier. "But I'm so ashamed of what I'm feeling, Bonnie." She glanced over her shoulder to be sure the child hadn't awakened and come into the kitchen. "Sometimes I'm so angry with her for coming into our lives and turning everything upside down." She shredded the tissue in her hands.

"You can't help what you feel," Bonnie soothed. "And your life has taken quite a shift. It can't be easy." Bonnie smiled and took Val's hands that were clutching the tissue. "Remember, feelings aren't good or bad, they're simply feelings. It's what you do with them that makes the difference… and you are doing everything right."

Val looked into her friend's eyes and knew it was true.

"Sometimes our lives get shaken up pretty badly. We don't know why, and it most certainly doesn't always seem fair, but even though we don't understand, God knows, and God will lead us through it."

Val realized Bonnie wasn't just talking about her situation. She was speaking of her own life, too. "Well, enough about me." Val tossed back her hair, lifted her chin, and forced a smile. "How's it going with your house? Have you heard anything back from the realtor about the prospective buyers? Or do you want to change your mind and move in here?" Val teased. She knew her friend was sure of her decision.

Bonnie laughed, but her face lit up with excitement. "They were approved and settlement is scheduled for the end of the month." She sighed and sat back in her chair. "It's hard letting go of our belongings though. I was glad the children took some things of Frank's with them when they went home, and of course, I have certain small treasures I'm holding onto, but I'm going to have to let go of a lot more since I'm downsizing." She took a deep breath as though she were about to share something more but stopped abruptly. "Oh hello, Betsy."

Val's head whipped around, and she saw the child standing shyly in the doorway clutching her blanket. *She looks so young, so tiny.*

"Hi, sweetheart. Are you feeling better?"

Betsy nodded but didn't move to come join them.

Val stood and went to her. "Miss Bonnie and I are having lunch. She also brought you some of your favorite chicken noodle soup. Would you like to try it?"

The five year old shook her head.

Betsy either talked a blue streak or didn't talk at all. Today, apparently, it would be the latter. She turned and headed back out of the kitchen while Val looked at her friend hopelessly. Her morose expression screamed, *See what I mean?*

Bonnie got up and started cleaning the lunch containers without a word.

"You don't have to do that, Bonnie."

"I know." She smiled, looking back from the sink. Within minutes everything had been cleared away, and Bonnie embraced her friend. "You know I pray for you and Andy and that little girl every night."

"Yes, I know. And I appreciate it. I continue to pray for God to comfort you and give you strength as well."

Hearing those words, Bonnie smiled at her dear friend. "And He does, my dear. He does. Whatever is going to happen here, He will carry you through it. Now, take care of yourself, and I'll talk to you tomorrow." They talked nearly every day now that Frank was gone.

Val closed the door behind Bonnie, hugged herself, and headed toward the guest room, unsure what might await her there.

CHAPTER TWENTY-FIVE

Bonnie stood at the door of her home, the home she and Frank had shared together. The home where they had raised their children, and where the children and grandchildren always gathered. *What will happen now?* But that home was already gone. It had been gone as soon as Frank was taken from her. It was gone before the young men from the Purple Heart had carried his chair out and put it on the truck. She knew donating that recliner was the right thing to do, but it felt almost like she was letting go of a piece of him. She had walked through each of the empty rooms and recalled the memories, but now it was time—time to say goodbye to that chapter and begin a new one.

She pulled the front door closed behind her and without looking back, walked to her car already parked in the driveway facing outward toward her next destination.

The real estate closing went smoothly, and she wished the young couple all the best in their new home. It seemed strange that a family of five would be occupying her home now. They had one son and two daughters. How ironic. They reminded her so much of her and Frank and Mark, Laura, and Beth. *It will be the perfect home for them, just as it was for us.*

When she arrived at her new cottage at the Masonic Village, Bonnie was surprised to find a note on the door. It was from Andy and Val. *"Welcome Home!"* it read. She smiled, unlocked the door, and saw the beautiful flowers that had been placed on her coffee table. Then she looked over toward the kitchen and saw a huge basket filled with all kinds of goodies—not one of those baskets made up professionally in a store—but made by Val and filled with what she knew Bonnie loved.

There was one bottle of red wine and a bottle of white, along with pasta, spaghetti sauce, and a bottle of olive oil and some parmesan cheese. There was also her favorite tea and a small box of chocolates.

What a great friend. Bonnie turned to get a bottle of water out of the refrigerator. She was glad she'd had time to stock her new home with necessities before moving in.

She walked from room to room, adjusting the thermostat just one degree warmer to take the chill from her bones, and found herself standing in the bedroom staring at the framed picture of a very young newlywed Frank and Bonnie. "Seems like yesterday," she murmured clutching the photo to her chest.

Returning the cherished image to its place on the nightstand, Bonnie meandered back to the living room and, with a sigh, eased herself into a chair by the window. Then she lifted her gaze and spied a beautiful cardinal sitting on the porch railing. He didn't fly away until Bonnie's wrinkled brow had softened and a slow smile lifted the corners of her mouth.

This will be okay. I'm going to be okay, Frank.

CHAPTER TWENTY-SIX

Sarah Reed looked at her stepdaughter's drawing. She wasn't sure exactly why it bothered her, but it did. She didn't know if she should ask her about it directly. They had a wonderful relationship, and she didn't want to do anything to jeopardize that so she decided to wait and talk to her husband instead. On impulse, she grabbed her cell phone and took a picture of the drawing.

It wasn't until all the children were asleep that she got the phone out and opened the picture. "Craig, would you take a look at this?" She showed him the picture and waited.

"Is this one of Mia's drawings?"

Sarah saw the crease between his brows deepen, and she answered quickly that it was.

After examining it for several more seconds, he added, "It's very dark, isn't it?"

"That's what I thought, but I didn't know what, if anything, I should do about it." She was sitting on the edge of the cushion next to her husband on the couch. "Do you think it's anything to be concerned about?"

"I'm not sure, hon, but I think it's worth having a conversation. What did she say when she showed it to you?"

"She didn't show it to me," Sarah admitted. "I was in the girls' room getting their dirty laundry before they came home from school, and I saw it on her drawing table. The combination of blues and purples drew me over. And then I saw the green eyes. And look, did you see this?"

Craig looked closely to the area of the picture Sarah was indicating. "Are those tears?" He tilted his head and looked at Sarah.

She saw the concern growing in his eyes. He looked back at the picture then in the direction of the stairs. Without another word, he rose and climbed the steps to the girls' bedroom. Sarah wondered if she should follow but decided to wait, hoping he wasn't going to wake Mia to ask her about it. Craig was usually pretty level-headed, and waking the child up would be a bit of an over-reaction.

She breathed a sigh of relief when she heard the faint sound of his footsteps coming back down the stairs. "Where did you go?"

"I looked in on the girls. They're both asleep." He smiled then. "Julie snores," he laughed, "just like her mother."

Sarah threw the couch pillow at his head but laughed with him. It wasn't the first time she'd heard about her snoring.

Craig didn't return his attention to the article he'd been reading in his golf magazine moments earlier. He sat very still looking at the floor, then slowly lifted his head and looked at his wife. "Do you think I should ask her about this tomorrow?"

"I wasn't sure at first, but yes, I think maybe you should say something. I mean you wouldn't have to tell her about your concerns, but if you happen to open a conversation, maybe she'll tell you what it means. She's always been happy to talk about her drawings in the past."

Craig nodded. "I'll tell her I saw it when I looked in on them tonight. I did, you know… after I looked at Mia and Julie sleeping like angels." He rolled his eyes and smiled. "It was still on her desk. The light from the hallway is bright enough that I could see it pretty clearly. She's really good, isn't she? Or is that a father's bias?"

"No, Craig, I don't think so. For a child her age, I believe she shows real talent, and her art teacher even told her she has great potential." Sarah saw the pride in her husband's eyes.

"Maybe she'll grow up to be a great artist," he crowed.

"Well I guess that's possible, Craig, but that's not her life's goal at the moment. She still says she wants to be a doctor so she can help soldiers when they get hurt fighting wars. Those commercials have really gotten to her."

Craig's eyes opened wider. "Do you think that might have something to do with the drawing?"

"Maybe." But Sarah had a hunch that wasn't it. She couldn't quite put her finger on it, but she sensed it was something more personal.

Craig turned his attention back to the journal he'd been reading. Sarah's thoughts, however, continued to focus on their four children. The two of them had been luckier than most with their blended family. Since the children were all so close in age, there could have been a lot of jealousy and rivalry rather than the friendships that had developed between them.

They argued and fought from time to time, of course, but it was like any siblings. Sarah knew it was, in part, because there had been no divorce involved. There were no other parents in the picture to drive wedges. Perhaps, Sarah thought, it was their shared grief that had bound them all together.

It was about an hour later that Sarah passed the girls' bedroom and heard crying. She pushed the door open gently and listened to see who it was. She couldn't tell which bed it was coming from so she tiptoed inside and found Mia crying into her pillow.

Sarah sat on the side of the bed and asked softly, "Mia, what is it? Are you okay?" The child didn't answer. "Are you not feeling well?"

Mia rolled over, sat up, and put her arms around her stepmother's neck. "I had an awful dream, Mom," she sobbed.

"Oh honey, I'm sorry. What was it about?" Sarah brushed the hair away from her face and saw Mia's puzzled look.

The girl sniffed and looked up into Sarah's eyes. "I don't know," she cried. She shook her head in confusion. "But it was so real, I mean, I knew a minute ago… and it was awful… but I don't remember anything now. I can't." Her face contorted in the effort.

"It's okay, sweetie. It's okay. That's the way dreams are sometimes." Sarah laid Mia back down and sat holding her hand until she heard the slow even breathing of sleep return. Then she gently tucked the covers in around her, took a look at her own daughter, Julie, who hadn't stirred, and quietly left the room.

"Where were you?" Craig asked when she finally reached their bedroom. He had already finished in the bathroom and was climbing into bed.

"Talking to Mia."

Craig's head snapped around. "You woke her up to ask about the drawing?" he asked incredulously.

"No, silly. I heard her crying and went in to see what was wrong." She saw the look of concern quickly etched on her husband's face and hurried to add, "Just a bad dream." Sarah explained that Mia couldn't remember what she'd dreamt.

"That's odd," Craig muttered. "She hasn't had any of those in years. Not since her mother was killed."

CHAPTER TWENTY-SEVEN

Susan walked out the door and through the gate, sucking in the fresh, frigid air. So glad to be out of that place, she wasn't even bothered by the stinging cold wind, at first.

She scanned the street. There was no one there to meet her. *Damn it! Miss Perfect promised!* Susan was furious and becoming more aware of the cold, She looked up and down the road. *Now what am I supposed to do?* She rubbed her hands together, then glad her bag had a long enough strap to hoist on her shoulder, balled them into fists and stuck them in her pockets. It felt like she'd never be warm again.

Susan had begged an old friend, from the bridge group she once played in, to pick her up. She was sure Bonnie wouldn't be able to say no. In Susan's mind, that woman was a goodie-two-shoes. But as Susan stood alone outside the prison, she began to doubt Bonnie was such a do-gooder after all. As much as she hated the idea, she was about to go back inside—a place she never wanted to enter again—when she saw a car come around the corner.

Thank God! She recognized Bonnie behind the wheel as the car got closer and she heaved a sigh of relief. Opening the passenger side door, Susan slid in, smiling sheepishly at her old friend. "Thanks for doing this, Bonnie. I really appreciate it," she said as she fastened her seatbelt.

Bonnie replied that she didn't mind, and asked how Susan was doing. *How am I doing? How do you think?* She could almost taste her own bitterness. "Okay, I guess," was all she said. She stared out the windshield and felt her insides begin to shake. *Why am I so nervous?*

Susan had refused to allow Elizabeth to visit her while she had been incarcerated. She missed her child, but didn't want the girl to see her mother in that setting. So, she'd settled for a few letters and phone calls instead.

Now she wondered if that had been a mistake. "Bonnie," she hated to ask but needed to know, "have you seen my little girl lately?"

A smile crossed the other woman's face. "Oh, of course. I see Betsy every time I go to Val's for Sunday dinner. She's doing just fine."

Susan resented the idea that Elizabeth would be doing just fine without her. "Her name is Elizabeth," she snapped.

Bonnie's face registered alarm.

Susan reined herself in and softened, "I'm... I'm sorry, but I've never been one for nicknames. We never shortened Elizabeth's name." *I've got to keep my cool with her—with all of them,* she admonished.

"Yes, I didn't mean to upset you, Susan. I've just gotten used to hearing her called that," Bonnie said apologetically.

"I'm not upset, Bonnie. I'm fine." *Why should I be upset... just because Val has my child and had the nerve to change her name!* She saw Bonnie's sidelong glance and put on her sweetest smile. "But I'm not sure why Val and Andy would give her a nickname at her age."

"Oh no, they didn't."

Susan was confused. "What do you mean? You said..."

"No, it wasn't Val or Andy who suggested the nickname. It was Bet... I mean Elizabeth."

"But... but why would she?" Susan stammered.

"Well, I don't know really."

Susan didn't believe her. *She's a shrink, and shrinks know everything, or at least they think they do.* Susan had spent her fair share of time with a psychiatrist while she had been locked up, and she hated every minute. She had learned what he wanted to hear, learned what she needed to say. She figured she worked him pretty good. The same way she worked all those fools in the AA meetings. *They might need that shit, but I don't.* She figured she had fooled them all. After all... she was out. She'd made parole.

"Susan, are you all right?" Bonnie asked.

Susan was startled out of her reverie, but didn't know how long Bonnie had been talking to her. "Oh yeah, sorry. I was thinking... what did you say again?"

"I asked for the address where you want me to take you."

"Oh, it's Maple Street. 800 Maple Street." Susan dreaded staying there, but she had no choice. The only way she got parole was by agreeing to go to a halfway house. More play-acting. She'd had about enough of it.

Bonnie finally pulled up in front of the address but didn't turn off the engine. Susan took that to mean she was anxious to get away. *I guess I'm not good enough for her now.*

Susan looked up at the big old house thinking it was probably once the home of a very wealthy family. This used to be one of the best neighborhoods in their small town. Now most of these mansions had been converted into offices for doctors or lawyers. Some were apartments.

This one was a halfway house. And for the next thirty days it would be like another prison. *Thirty meetings in thirty days,* she thought. *Whatever.*

Susan looked at Bonnie with a half-smile. "Well, I don't want to keep you. Anyway, I need to get registered, and I'm sure you're anxious to get home to Frank."

Susan grabbed the small bag she'd thrown in the back seat, and headed up the front walk to her new home. She looked back over her shoulder and watched Bonnie drive away. In that moment, she hated her old 'friend' for being so normal.

CHAPTER TWENTY-EIGHT

onnie struggled to see the road through the blur of her tears, and soon pulled into a strip mall until she could get control. She didn't normally break down like this, but Susan's comment had caught her completely off-guard. It had never occurred to her that Susan wouldn't have heard about Frank's death. And when she made that comment, it was like no time had passed at all. Like she had just lost him all over again.

It doesn't seem to be getting any easier, Frank.

She blew her nose, put the car in gear and headed home. She would barely have time to shower and dress. It was Thursday, and Thursday was bridge night. Bonnie looked forward to Thursdays now more than ever. She managed to fill many of her afternoons and several evenings a week. Every Tuesday she had choir practice, Wednesday afternoon was Bible study, and she had the occasional lunch with Judy or one of her other friends. Then of course, there was lunch with Val once or twice a week now, and she knew she had an open invitation to Sunday dinner at their house—or at Craig and Sarah's when the Reeds all gathered there. But bridge night was special.

Even when she stayed at home, Bonnie kept herself occupied with reading and working on her memoir. It was the one thing she wanted to leave her children more than anything else. Something she hoped they would treasure. A look at their parents' love story and their beginnings.

Normally *days* weren't the problem, with the exception of a punch in the stomach now and then like the one Susan had given her. Nights were more difficult. Though she read until she was drowsy before even heading to bed, then read her devotions and said her prayers until exhausted, there were still times when she lay awake for hours. When she'd downsized to the cottage from their big old house, she had wisely brought some of the most meaningful pieces with her. Aside from Frank's favorite chair. She couldn't look at it without feeling the pain of its emptiness and decided to bring smaller pieces of him to her new home.

Each time she entered her cottage, the first thing she saw upon opening the door, was their family portrait. That was one of her most cherished possessions. Bonnie and Frank were seated side by side. Beth, who had been only five years old at the time, was sitting on her mother's lap. Seven-year-old Laura stood close by her mother's side, and nine-year-old Mark was beside his father.

There were many, many more portraits adorning the walls of her new cottage. Bonnie loved all the pictures of the children and had placed photos of their biggest days all on one wall. First was Mark's college graduation and his wedding picture. Below and centered under that was a picture of Laura on her graduation day. Bonnie thought perhaps someday she might be able to add a wedding picture there, too… only time would tell. Then below that was a picture of Beth's graduation and the day she'd married Adam. These were all precious to Bonnie, but the portraits that were the most personal and both warmed and squeezed her heart were hung in the bedroom.

The first one was her wedding picture. She looked at it now and reminisced at how young and how in love they had been. She had been twenty-three and Frank was twenty-five. Dressed in white with long raven-black hair, she was standing next to the love of her life, so handsome in his tux. *We had no idea the adventures ahead of us, did we, dear?*

Next to that, and cherished as dearly, was the picture Laura had taken on their twenty-fifth wedding anniversary. *I thought—and hoped— we'd make it to our fiftieth.*

"All right, Bonnie. You'd better quit lollygagging and get your shower," she said aloud. "Great, now I'm talking to myself." *Well there's no one else to talk to.*

Moments later she was struck with an idea. *A companion!* Amazingly, the very thought raised her spirits.

Fresh from the shower and dressed for the bridge game at Sarah Reed's house tonight, Bonnie looked at the time and grabbed her iPad to check out some websites. There were questions to be decided like age and background. The excitement of the possibilities totally occupied her mind.

After half an hour exploring the internet, Bonnie thought she had narrowed it down to a choice between three. She wanted a good match for a person of her age and habits.

My goodness, she thought, *there are so many to choose from.* Reading the descriptions, Bonnie's excitement grew. They seemed to come in all shapes and sizes, and Bonnie was amazed at how cute some of the older ones still were. Many descriptions read "quiet," or "friendly"—the latter was certainly crucial—and one seemed remarkably intelligent. *I like that.*

But Bonnie found herself especially drawn to the last one that said, "…likes to take long walks but is also okay with alone time." *So, I could still do the things I enjoy, like playing bridge.*

She easily ruled out the first one because there seemed to be a lot of health problems. It was down to a choice between two—one very handsome specimen and a second that was terribly cute. She glanced at the time on her phone and was surprised by how long she'd been absorbed in her search.

It was time to get going or they would be trying to play bridge with three people—which never works. Grabbing her purse and keys, Bonnie headed for the car. She had lots of news to share.

CHAPTER TWENTY-NINE

When she pulled into the driveway, Bonnie smiled. She wasn't the only one who had gone through a big change lately.

Craig and Sarah had moved into a big beautiful house with much more room for their family. When they first got married, the house Craig had shared with Jenny still seemed to work. But now as a family of six, more room made sense.

When the children were little they loved sharing rooms—it was a long never-ending sleepover. But now the kids were getting older and needed their space.

Craig and Sarah had talked about how nice it would be if each of the children had their own room, especially when they became teenagers... and particularly the girls. Cody and Bobby Jr. said they really didn't need separate rooms—but that could certainly change with age.

The couple had planned to expand five years ago when Sarah became pregnant, but after she lost the child, it hurt too much to think about. Eased by time, and with the children almost teens, they had revisited those plans. Plus, thanks to the change in Sarah's career status, they could finally afford the house of their dreams.

And it's their house.

Bonnie knew Sarah had never once complained about living in the home Craig had shared with Jenny, but she did wonder if Jenny's ghost wasn't everywhere, much the way Frank's had haunted her.

Now as Bonnie sat in her car looking up at the warm glow from the windows, she allowed a moment of nostalgia while remembering her own home with her three young children filling it with laughter... and tears... but mostly laughter. She prayed a short blessing for the family living inside before going up the path to the entrance.

The door was ajar, so she knocked gently and went on in.

"Hello?" She was greeted by Sarah who swept her through the entry, and several other beautiful rooms before landing in the spacious family room where the others were already snacking and chatting.

Bonnie joined in but noticed secretive looks exchanged between Val and Sarah. Her curiosity finally got the best of her. "All right, what's going on here?" she asked looking from one to the other.

Kathy, who hadn't noticed the exchanges looked surprised and curious.

Since there was no denial forthcoming, Bonnie continued, "You two look like a couple of cats who've swallowed canaries. Give…"

"You don't miss much, do you, Bonnie?" Sarah smiled and winked at her mother-in-law whose grin was a mile wide. "Okay, I do have news, and I wanted to wait until we were all here together to share it."

"Well?" Kathy asked excitedly. She loved gossip more than anyone, especially if it was news she could share.

Then Bonnie had a thought. "You're not?" her eyes went wide and got even wider when Sarah nodded.

"What?" Kathy almost shouted.

Sarah looked at her young friend and finally spilled the beans. "Craig and I are going to have a baby."

The room exploded with joy and hugs all around. Their youngest children were the boys, who were both eight years old, and the girls were ten and eleven now, so a baby would certainly make a huge change in the household.

"Have you told the children?" Bonnie wondered how they would take the news.

"Yes," Sarah answered still beaming. "The girls are thrilled and beside themselves with thoughts of having a baby sister. Cody, of course, wants a little brother, and Bobby Jr. says he doesn't care."

Bonnie noticed a deepening between her brows.

"I don't think Bobby Jr.'s quite as enthusiastic about the idea as the others."

He's been your baby for a long time, Bonnie thought, but simply said, "I'm sure he'll come around… Maybe you should have a boy to increase the odds."

The women all laughed and decided to start their game though they were more excited about the pregnancy than the cards.

It was at least an hour later, when the baby talk had run its course, that Bonnie decided to make her own announcement. "Well, Sarah, I have some news, too." When she had everyone's attention, she smiled slyly and added, "You're not the only one who's going to have an addition to her family." Then she looked from one dumbfounded face to another and said, "I'm getting a puppy."

CHAPTER THIRTY

Susan was furious. The woman at the hospital was beyond rude. She had the nerve to say 'good luck' after not giving her any chance of getting her job back. Susan hated her. She hated all of those self-righteous people out there. *Well, screw them. Screw them all!*

She sat in the car she'd rented with a fake ID wondering what to do. What kind of job could a nurse who's also an ex-convict get? They said there were steps she could take to get her nursing license back, but it would be a long, slow process. Yet her parole and halfway house rules said she needed to get a job now.

Susan was devastated and feeling sorry for herself—a common state of affairs ever since her husband had left. *Damn you, Marty!* Everything that had gone wrong in her life was his fault. Holding tight to the steering wheel to steady her shaky hands, Susan stared at the storefront across from her. She checked the rearview mirror before getting out of the car and walking the short distance to the liquor store.

Going straight to the aisle where the vodka was lined up on shelf after shelf, Susan found her favorite Smirnoff and grabbed the bottle in both hands. When she passed the row of Scotches on the way to the register, her eyes lingered on the Glenlivet. But that was out of the question. Both the cost and the telltale smell it would leave on her breath ruled that out. The Smirnoff would have to do.

Susan made the purchase with her limited funds, then looked up and down the street before heading back to the car. She wanted a drink right away. She needed a drink badly... but not yet. She held tight to the steering wheel and drove off the lot. The vodka, in its plain brown bag, was tucked under the passenger seat.

After what seemed like an endless drive, Susan parked her car on the shaded lane leading to the lake. She got out and walked down to the very bench she'd once shared with Andy Reed. That was so long ago... or was it? The child conceived during their little tryst was five years old now… or was she six? Susan couldn't think clearly. She took a couple of big gulps from the bottle in the brown bag. There was no one around except the man on the bridge, and he was too far away to see what she was doing, as if he'd care. *No one really cares.*

She thought again of Elizabeth. Thought about the way the child had looked at her earlier in the day. She had stood by Val's side and not spoken a word until Susan finally said, "Come here, Elizabeth." And even then, she had hesitated. Once she finally came over, Elizabeth had accepted her hug and hugged her back, but seemed apprehensive.

"Why don't you tell your momma how you're doing in school, Betsy?" Val had said.

"Her name is Elizabeth!" Susan had snapped. And she remembered being rebuked by her own little girl.

"Momma, don't be mad. I told her to call me that."

Susan remembered how the child had clammed up when she'd asked why. She remembered how her daughter had clung to her when the time was up and she had to leave. She remembered the sadness in those five-year-old eyes.

It was getting dark, and Susan knew she should be getting back to the house before curfew, but she wasn't ready to face them. She wasn't ready for another stupid AA meeting either. She thought about her counselor, Nancy. *Hmph. I don't need her. I don't need any of them or their stupid Serenity Prayer.* She put the bottle to her lips, but it was dry. Tossing it into the trash bin near the bench, she staggered back to her rental car.

Susan knew she shouldn't be driving, but she didn't care. She put the key in the ignition and started the engine.

♥

The man on the bridge saw her stagger over to the dark-colored car. He shook his head in disbelief when she got in and he heard the engine start. "Boy, that's one dumb broad!" he muttered. "Somebody ought to stop her before she gets hurt."

CHAPTER THIRTY-ONE

Val was glad Bonnie didn't have any plans for the evening, and Andy had taken Betsy for a play date with Mia. In spite of the big age difference, the two girls loved spending time together. Mia was like a little mother. And Betsy craved the attention. Andy agreed that a visit with Mia might be the best medicine for a little girl with the blues. And Val really needed to talk to her best friend about Susan's visit.

Bonnie met her at the door with Ginger in her arms. Val thought the little Pomeranian was the perfect companion and could see Bonnie had already fallen madly in love.

"Come in, dear. You sounded upset when you called. Is everything okay?"

Val was quick to reassure her everyone was all right, then added that it was about her foster child—Andy's little girl. "You should have seen her face, Bonnie. I mean, first I didn't even think Betsy was going to go to her mother. She was kind of almost hiding behind me—and Susan looked daggers at me—like it was my fault. Can you imagine?" Val shook her head in frustration. "And when she did go to her she hardly talked at all. It was all just so awkward!"

"I can only imagine. That poor child has been through so much, but at least she's had you and Andy to give her some stability until Susan can get herself straightened out."

"If she ever does." Val rolled her eyes. "Honestly, I'm trying not to be judgmental, but the woman's changed. And she about snapped my head off when I made a mistake of using the nickname Betsy."

"Oh, I should have warned you about that."

Val raised her eyebrows. "What do you mean?"

Bonnie told her about the exchange they had the day Susan was released from prison.

"That's right," Val tilted her head, "I had forgotten you got roped into picking her up." Val wanted to be charitable, but was finding it very difficult. "I'm sorry, but it's just not fair, you know? I mean it's not Betsy's fault her mother is an alcoholic, but she's paying the price… *and so am I.*"

Bonnie didn't say anything for a moment, and the silence was thick with defeat.

Bonnie finally broke the silence. "Could we pray together?"

Val brushed away the tears of frustration and gave her hands to her friend.

"Lord, we come to you to ask for your help for our little Betsy."

Val felt calmer driving home, and was much more in control by the time Andy and his daughter got there. Andy carried his little girl, already half asleep, straight to the bedroom. Val waited for her husband to return and asked how the visit had gone. "Did she cheer up once she got to see Mia?"

"Not right away." Andy sat down with a heavy sigh. "I didn't think she was ever going to snap out of it, but eventually she and Mia went off together, and we left them alone for a while. Then Craig went to check on them." He looked up at Val wistfully. "We raised a pretty special man, Val," he said, and Val noticed his glassy eyes as he fought back tears. "He seems to have forgiven his old man, and I wouldn't have blamed him if he never had." He sniffed and cleared his throat, "But anyhow, Craig said when he listened at the door, which was slightly ajar, he heard Mia praying. He peeked in and she was holding Betsy's hands and praying with her. Isn't that amazing?"

Val nodded. "I'd say that special man we managed to raise is doing a pretty darned good job of raising a remarkable young lady. What were they praying about?"

"Craig didn't stay to listen. He said he felt guilty listening in… but I wish he had. I wondered the same thing."

"Do you think we should ask her? Mia, I mean… not Betsy."

"I don't know.

Meanwhile, in another part of town, a driver slammed on the brakes. But not in time.

Chapter Thirty-Two

onnie and Ginger came in after their walk, and both went for a drink of water.

"You were pretty thirsty weren't you, my little Gingersnap." The dog followed her to the sitting room and immediately jumped in her lap when she sat down. "That's my girl."

Bonnie was amazed by how quickly they had bonded. Her little Pomeranian was already six months old when she got her. The puppy's previous owner's grandchild had terrible allergies and had given her up. When Bonnie heard about the situation, it seemed meant to be. She called and went to meet Ginger. It was love at first sight—for both of them.

"Shall we see what's going on in the world, little one?" Ginger put her chin on Bonnie's chest and winked up at her. Their walk had her tuckered out, so it was time for a nap.

Bonnie picked up the remote and clicked on the "Today Show." She watched for a few moments and then switched to the local news brief on the half hour.

"Hit-and-run driver leaves pedestrian in critical condition. Anyone who has information on this incident is asked to contact Madison police."

Bonnie shook her head unable to understand how anyone could leave someone lying on the street to die.

The TV droned on while Bonnie said, "I think we got our walk in just in time, Ginger. The weather guy says rain will be moving in by nine o'clock this morning." Ginger lifted her little head to give her best friend a kiss. "Yes, I love you too… yes, I do."

Bonnie felt a closeness to Ginger, more than she even had with Molly, the wonderful collie she and Frank had for almost fifteen years. But Molly was Frank's dog… especially after he retired. Since he walked her every day, and fed her, she followed him around and laid at his feet.

She and Frank had always loved collies—never even considered any other breed—but Ginger was perfect for Bonnie at this stage of life, and had stolen her heart. Just holding the soft, little pup was comforting. She looked down at that sweet face and couldn't resist doing what all the younger people did all the time—reached for her phone to take a selfie. She wished her arms were a little longer, but she got it, and chuckled at the result. *Val has got to see this.*

She IM'd the picture with a message, "Me and my new best friend."

Seconds later, she heard the whoosh of a reply. "Oh no, I've been replaced."

"Never," she answered adding a wink emoji. With that, her cell phone rang, and she accepted the call immediately.

"Well good morning, Val, and no Ginger could never replace you." Her friend laughed on the other end of the line. "But Ginger is my cuddle-up friend. Honestly, she was the best cure for what ailed me. I don't feel so alone in this place anymore, and I actually have someone to talk to from the time I get up until I go to bed."

"I'm so glad. So how would you and Ginger feel about a little company this morning?"

"Well, I don't know. Let me check with her." She looked at Ginger, still trying to nap, and asked, "Hey girl, would you like some company?" Then she answered Val, "I have a wagging little tail here that says yes, she'd like that. And so would I!"

Bonnie knew what time Val took Betsy to her school bus so she had the tea ready. She poured and added a little sugar and milk, the way she'd learned to drink it on her visit to London many years before.

Val had stopped at Starbucks on her way and picked up some of their favorite lemon pound cake, so Bonnie grabbed a couple of plates. It was the fine china she used daily with her philosophy of 'What am I saving it for?'

"To what do I owe this unexpected visit?" Bonnie couldn't help but worry with all the upheaval of late.

Val smiled. "You know me too well, girlfriend." She stirred her tea and took a moment before answering. "This may sound strange, but something happened with Betsy last night, and I'm not sure what to make of it."

"That child has been through so much. What now?"

Val explained she had put Betsy to bed around nine o'clock, and she was sound asleep when she looked in on her at ten. "But when I was heading to bed myself, I thought I heard a noise coming from her bedroom so I stopped to listen. I realized she was praying—not that I found that disturbing, although it was strange for her to be asleep and then wake up and say her prayers—but it's what she was asking that was peculiar."

"What was it?" Bonnie leaned forward in anticipation.

"She said something like 'please don't let the old man die' and 'It wasn't her fault.' I didn't want to intrude so when I heard her say amen and crawl back into bed, I just tiptoed to my room. I didn't say anything to Andy—maybe I should have—but he's been stressed enough lately, and I didn't want to add to it." Val looked at Bonnie, head tilted and said, "It's probably nothing, right?"

"Probably." Bonnie leaned back in her chair, unconsciously scratching her ginger-colored friend behind the ears. "Maybe you should ask her about it though."

"Oh, I did. This morning on the way to the bus stop I told her I overheard her praying for an old man last night... and I quickly assured her I hadn't meant to eavesdrop, that I was just on my way to bed and heard her. But she looked at me like she had absolutely no idea what I was talking about."

"Really? That is strange."

"That's what I thought, too. But she seemed certain I was dreaming or something. She told me she said her prayers before she went to sleep, just like Mia taught her," Val smiled when she said that, "but that she didn't know any old man. Isn't that weird? I mean, do you think she was dreaming so vividly that she was talking in her sleep?"

"I don't know, Val. I really don't." Bonnie refilled their cups and added, "But it does make you wonder what old man she could be dreaming about—or what the old man represents to her—and who the 'she' might be?"

"Indeed it does. And what didn't she mean to happen…"

Chapter Thirty-Three

Susan woke up confused in unfamiliar surroundings. She was curled up, shivering on the ground with her coat wrapped tightly around her. Her head ached and she was shocked to see dried blood on her hands.

Looking around, she found her opened purse on the ground a few feet away and dug for her compact. One look in the mirror showed where the blood had come from. There was a long, jagged cut across her forehead which stung and began to bleed again when she touched it.

Searching for a tissue, she realized her wallet was gone. *What the hell?* She looked around and struggled to her feet. There was no one in sight. *How did I get here? What's going on?* she wondered. She was in a wooded area far from the part of the park she knew.

"Damn it! Somebody took my damn wallet." Then she saw something on the ground a little farther away than where she'd found her purse. She hurried toward it, thinking it was the missing wallet, but her feet couldn't keep up with the rest of her body and she met the ground— hard. Steadying herself, she crawled closer and discovered it was just a rock. "Damn it!" she cried again. The little bit of money she'd had was in that wallet, and now even that was gone. "Well at least they didn't get much," she muttered bitterly.

But how did I get here, and why can't I remember?

She remembered seeing Elizabeth but what happened after that wasn't clear… and she was so cold. She found her way to a path and followed it in the direction she hoped would get her out of wherever she was and finally came to a clearing and a more familiar part of the park. Far in the distance she saw a bridge and vaguely remembered seeing it last night. *But how did I get here?* There was no one sitting on the bench, or anywhere in sight for that matter, so she made her way over to it and sat down, pulling her coat tightly around her and shoving her hands in the pockets.

Slowly bits and pieces came back of the night before. There was a rental car, yes, and she'd driven it here… but first she'd made a stop. Susan groaned aloud.

"Vodka. Oh God, yes, I stopped and got a bottle of Smirnoff," she muttered. But that's the last thing she remembered. She didn't remember drinking it. She didn't remember anything. *And where in the hell is that car?* She thought about going back to the rental place but was afraid. She looked up at the bare tree limbs stretching into the gray sky and knew she couldn't sit there much longer or she'd freeze her butt off. Her entire body shook uncontrollably.

Susan saw a young woman jogging toward her and tried to get up. She didn't want anyone to see her like this. But when she began to stand she found herself unsteady and took a moment to get her balance. By then the twenty-something woman was close enough to see the shape she was in.

"Are you okay, Miss? Do you need help?" The woman had slowed down and was stopping right in front of her.

Susan's embarrassment came out as anger. "No! I don't need any help. Leave me alone."

The young woman threw both arms up, said 'sorry' in a voice that obviously indicated she wasn't, and jogged away with one more glance over her shoulder at the crazy woman.

Then Susan thought of the halfway house and her curfew. *Oh no, oh my gosh… I'm in big trouble.* She tried to think of a way out. This could land her back in her cell. *No, I've got to think of something.* She had managed to walk to the edge of the park and saw a convenience store less than a block away. There was a bathroom there where she could clean up a little and finally get out of the cold.

By the time she reached it, she had begun to formulate a story to explain why she hadn't gotten back there last night. Seeing the gash on her forehead it all became clear. *I'll tell them I was mugged. Yeah, someone hit me in the head, grabbed my purse, took my wallet and what little money I had. And who knows, that might even be true…*

Fortunately, they hadn't taken her phone so once she was cleaned up, she called the number of the halfway house, gave them the brief version of what happened, explained she was hurt, and said she needed a ride.

Susan gave them her location, and the woman on the other end of the line said she'd send someone to get her. It turned out to be one of the women in charge—the one she disliked the most. Chelsea was so discerning it scared her. Susan feared she would see right through her story and call her parole officer. She needn't have worried.

"Oh jeeze, Susan, that's a pretty deep gash. I think you're going to need stitches." Chelsea insisted on taking her to get it looked at before going back to the halfway house.

Meanwhile, Susan realized she was starving and feeling sick to her stomach. She fought back the nausea the best she could but had to open the window to get some air.

Chelsea looked at her strangely. "Are you okay?" she asked solicitously.

Susan was getting sicker and more paranoid. *What if she suspects?* "No, I'm fine."

"I don't think so."

Susan began to shake inside. *She doesn't believe me.*

"Susan, you might have a concussion. We definitely need to have a doctor look at you."

Susan let out her breath in relief and agreed.

When the urgent care nurse was cleaning out the wound so the doctor could stitch it up, Susan felt her knees go weak and everything went white. The nurse told her to take slow, deep breaths. This was turning out all right. Everyone was feeling sorry for her. She decided it would be okay... until the doctor came in.

"So how did you say this happened, Ms. Walters?" Susan restated the story she had told Chelsea, and was startled when the doctor asked, "Did you call the police yet?"

"What?" Susan felt her stomach flip flop.

"You need to report this attack. Maybe the police can catch the scumbag who did this to you." Susan tried to be still as he continued to sew and talk. "Not much chance you'll get your money back though. I hope you weren't carrying a lot of cash with you."

"No," Susan said not much above a whisper. "He didn't get much. It's not that big a deal."

"Of course it is," the young doctor said. "Don't try to be a hero. Remember you're the victim here, and nobody should have to go through an experience like that."

Yeah, that's right, she thought, *I'm the victim!*

CHAPTER THIRTY-FOUR

Val had just returned home from her visit with Bonnie when she got the phone call. Seeing the school number on her caller ID, she dreaded answering. "Here we go again," she muttered.

Val waited for the nurse's voice to give her the usual message that Betsy complained of a stomachache.

"Mrs. Reed? This is Miss Rhen." It wasn't the nurse. It was Betsy's teacher. Val realized she had been holding her breath. "I'm afraid we have a problem with Elizabeth."

"What's wrong? What happened?" Val felt her heart thumping madly. "Is she all right?"

"Oh yes, I mean she's not hurt or anything, but she had a little accident." There was a slight pause then the teacher continued apologetically. "She must have waited too long to ask to use the bathroom, and she wet her pants."

"Oh no! I'm so sorry!" Val didn't know what else to say.

"Please don't feel bad, Mrs. Reed. Betsy's not the first student to ever have an accident. The nurse keeps some pants on hand for those mishaps, so she fixed her up."

So why are you calling me?

"The problem is that she won't come back to the classroom, and she won't talk to anybody. She has totally clammed up. She's probably embarrassed because some of the other children saw what happened and laughed. I talked to them about how inappropriate that was," she hurried to add, "and I explained that to Elizabeth, but she won't respond."

"I can be there in twenty minutes." Val was already grabbing her purse and keys and heading for the door.

"All right, I appreciate it. But take your time, she'll be fine, and she's waiting in the nurse's office. My lunch break is over and I have to get back to my classroom."

♥

When Val got to the school, she found Betsy sitting curled up in a chair in the corner of the nurse's suite sucking her thumb. As the weeks went by, the girl seemed to be regressing more and more. The thumb-sucking hadn't been apparent when she'd first moved in with them, but now she was seeing it frequently.

Val signed her out and took the bag of wet clothes from the nurse.

Back in the car, Betsy remained mute staring out the side window.

Val attempted to draw her out. "Nobody is mad at you, you know, sweetie." No answer. "And your teacher told me it's not that unusual for children to have accidents. It could happen to anyone." She kept sneaking looks at the sad little face in the rearview mirror. A tear crept down the side of her face. "Are you okay, baby?"

"I'm not a baby," Betsy cried.

"No, no you're not. I didn't mean it that way. It's just a nickname, like sweetie or honey." *I am such an idiot. I couldn't have thought of a worse thing to say.* Val glanced in the mirror again. Betsy looked furious.

When they got back to the house, the child ran straight to her room and slammed the door behind her. Val knew by now that meant she needed alone time. She stared at the closed door and ran her fingers back through her hair in utter frustration.

When Craig was a child, he had been so easy. Nothing like this. Once he was potty-trained, he never had an accident. He didn't have tantrums or act out. He was just an easy-going little boy. *But then, his mother never got drunk, put him in the car, had an accident, and wound up in prison. And his father didn't up and leave one day.* Val understood that this little girl had plenty of reason to be messed up—but she simply didn't know how to help.

Andy's the psychologist. He should be dealing with this, not me.

Val tried not to get angry, but like her husband always said, feelings aren't right or wrong. They're just feelings. It's what you do about them that counts. And she was certainly doing everything she could. But it wasn't enough. It was his turn to deal with his daughter. She went to the study, closed the door, and picked up her phone.

"Call me when you get this message…" she said. "It's about your daughter."

♥

"You're the psychologist… and her father! You need to step up." Val's frustration had reached her voice, and she saw the shock in her husband's eyes after he came home for the day. "Look, I'm sorry, but I feel like I'm in over my head, and… and I don't want to sound insensitive, but this shouldn't all fall on me."

"You're right, Val, and I'm sorry." Andy wrapped his arms around her, and Val felt herself begin to relax. She hadn't realized how tense every muscle in her body had become.

Then she felt the tears start. She hadn't meant to cry. But the tears came unbidden.

Andy pulled her closer. "Oh, sweetheart, please don't cry. We'll figure this out."

"No, I'm okay," she said, "I don't know why the tears. I'm just really tired, I guess."

Andy lifted her chin and wiped away the tear running down her cheek with his other hand. "Listen, you're going to go to your bridge group tonight, and I'm going to stay right here with Betsy. I'll call Craig and tell him we're going to skip the visit this week, okay?"

Val thought about it and wondered if the children would be disappointed not to get to visit. "Are you sure that won't upset her more? She always looks forward to spending time with Mia."

"Yes, you're right. Okay, how 'bout this—we'll go over and let the kids visit, but she and I won't stay as long. After an hour, I'll bring her home, we'll have ice cream, and then I'll talk with her—see what I can find out."

Val sighed, feeling a huge weight had been taken off her shoulders. She wrapped her arms around her husband's neck. "Thank you, Andy. Sorry I yelled at you." And she was—sort of—but a part of her hoped he'd remember everything.

CHAPTER THIRTY-FIVE

Susan paced the floor in her room back at the halfway house. She unconsciously reached up and touched the bandage on her forehead. Her head had stopped throbbing, leaving her with nothing but a dull ache.

Why can't I remember? She held her hands out in front of her and saw how they trembled. Unable to stop them, she went to her bed and sat on them. *Oh God, I need a drink. But there's nothing in this place, and there's no way I can leave anymore tonight.* It had been a long day… a lot of hours since she woke up in the park, lost and confused.

Even though she hadn't had breakfast or lunch, she had struggled to eat at the dinner table. Her stomach churned when she even thought about food.

Seven o'clock... It was almost time for the AA meeting at the church on the corner. They all usually gathered by twenty after and started the meeting promptly at 7:30. Susan hated those meetings. *I'm not like those women.* Susan never thought of herself as an alcoholic—she liked to drink—but she didn't *have* to drink. She had never blacked out before— not really. Sure, she thought, there were times she didn't remember everything… things were a little fuzzy maybe… but that wasn't like blacking out, not really.

But this time was different. No matter how hard she tried, she couldn't remember a thing after buying her Smirnoff. *What the hell happened to me? And where did I leave that car?*

Susan dragged herself to the meeting, and listened when the first woman began to share. "My name is Theresa and I'm an alcoholic," she said.

"Hi Theresa," everyone responded.

"I have been clean and sober for six months. When I drink, I do things that hurt the people I love." Theresa went on to say how she'd stolen from her parents in order to get money for her drugs and booze, and how she had ruined her last relationship by getting drunk and going home with a different man.

Susan listened to Theresa. For the first time in one of these meetings, she actually listened. And then she thought about it. She wanted to stand up and tell them everything. For the first time, she wanted to unburden herself. To tell the truth. To finally honestly acknowledge the truth of it.

But she couldn't. She was glued to the chair. Two more people took their turns and still Susan hesitated. *What am I going to say? What did I do last night?* She knew they wouldn't judge her, yet she was paralyzed—completely unable to take those few steps to the front of the room.

At the close of the meeting, when they said the Serenity Prayer, Susan spoke the words intentionally for the first time in her life. *God, grant me the serenity to accept the things I cannot change, courage to change the things I can, and wisdom to know the difference.*

Afterward there were snacks and beverages, but Susan sat immobilized in her seat, simply unable to move. She finally followed as some of the women slowly drifted out of the meeting room and headed home or, like Susan, back to the halfway house. When they got back, someone turned the TV on and two other women settled in to relax and watch. Susan's rubbery legs got her as far as the chair in the corner where she dissolved.

She saw the light from the TV, heard the voices, but was lost in her own thoughts… that is, until the news bulletin.

"…Hit-and-run… victim is in critical condition. Car believed to be a dark blue or black sedan probably with damage to the front end and a broken right headlight… any information, contact the Madison County Police Department."

Susan stared wide-eyed at the TV. She hadn't heard all of it, but she'd heard "hit-and-run." She heard "victim in critical condition." And she heard the description of a car that could have been the one she was driving last night. *No! There are lots of dark colored sedans. It wasn't me. It couldn't have been me! But damn it—what happened to that car?*

Susan felt sick. She bolted out of her chair with a sudden shot of adrenalin and ran back up to her room, slamming the door behind her.

Thank God, Penny's not here anymore. Penny was her roommate, but she had served the time required, done well, and been released two days earlier. Susan leaned against the door then dashed across the hall to the bathroom and threw up the little bit left in her stomach.

She was shaky and totally drained when she got back to her room and not at all in the mood for company, but Nancy came up beside her as she reached for the doorknob.

"Susan, can we talk for a little while?"

Susan tried to get rid of her, explaining she wasn't feeling too well.

"I know," Nancy said. "I've been there. I know the signs."

"What? What do you mean?"

"It's okay," Nancy said in a whisper, "I'm not going to rat you out. I just want to talk for a few minutes… then I'll leave, I promise."

Susan looked up and down the hall, then opened the door and followed her new friend inside, closing the door behind them. "I don't know what you're talking about, Nancy." Susan went over and sat on the side of her bed knowing her legs were about to give way from beneath her. "I was mugged last night, and I guess I had a mild concussion so I'm just kind of sick."

"Uh-huh, and very shaky. I saw how your hands were shaking downstairs." She sat down next to Susan on the bed and put a hand on her back. "It's okay. I know… I heard what happened to you, and I'm really sorry, but I don't think that's all that happened, is it?"

"I don't know what you're talking about." Susan felt panicky and wiped her sweaty palms on her jeans.

"I'm saying you look like you need a drink real bad." She moved closer and put her arm around Susan speaking softly. "I've been there. I understand. I only want to help… if I can."

Susan didn't answer. Her mind was spinning.

"Whenever you're ready, Susan. Just know I'm here."

The next morning Susan woke up at first light in spite of not getting to sleep for hours. She figured she may have slept a total of two, maybe three hours all night. But she couldn't lie there for one more minute. Gathering her toiletries, she headed for the bathroom.

Half an hour later she was showered, dressed and headed downstairs to get online. A quick search and she found what she'd been looking for. There still weren't a lot of details, and it didn't give the man's name, but she learned he was seventy-one years old, a father and grandfather, and he was still listed as critical but stable.

Susan was a nurse. She knew what that meant, and she was scared. She logged off the computer and retreated to her room. She could hear the other women stirring now. It wouldn't be long until breakfast, but Susan still had no appetite.

She took out the one possession she'd carried with her ever since her incarceration—the picture of the most important person in her life, Elizabeth. She ran her finger over her beautiful child's image. "My sweet Elizabeth," she whispered, "I'm so sorry. I'm so, so sorry." Then she fell to her knees. *God, help me. Forgive me. I'm so sorry. I didn't mean to hurt anybody. Please forgive me."* Everything Susan had ever learned about the God she believed in told her He was a forgiving God. But could she forgive herself?

What if he dies? Oh God, what if I killed someone? Please don't let him die!

CHAPTER THIRTY-SIX

Ginger sniffed the grass every few feet.

"Come on, Gingersnap. It's a bit nippy out here. Enough lollygagging. Let's do what we came for and get back inside and get warm." Bonnie didn't used to mind the cold quite so much. She'd never loved it, but these days, she felt it in her bones. However, Ginger was not to be rushed.

It had begun to snow, and the dog was fascinated by the phenomenon. Bonnie decided there was no choice but to accept so she might as well make the most of it. She breathed in and felt the cold in her nostrils... Tasted it... Savored it. She looked around and could still see the green grass. Not terribly green, but the dull brownish green of winter. But this morning each blade had donned a tiny white snowflake hat.

It began snowing harder, and Bonnie's little Teacup Pomeranian started snapping at the snowflakes. She loved her new game so it took a while before she remembered the purpose of their walk and decided to take care of business. The flakes kept getting larger and coming faster.

"Come on, Ginger. We'd better be getting back before this snow swallows you up." It wasn't many more steps before the pup signaled she really wasn't enjoying this walk anymore. She wanted to be carried... and of course Bonnie complied. She wasn't sure which one of them was becoming better trained.

"What's the matter, little one? Don't like walking on this white stuff? Are your little paws getting cold?" It felt good holding her. "I don't blame you, girl. I don't like it either. Let's get back inside." Fortunately, they didn't have far to go, and they were both happy to be back in the nice warm cottage.

Before long they were snuggled up together on the couch. Ginger had been given her treat, and Bonnie contentedly sipped her tea. Even though she wasn't crazy about the cold, she always felt invigorated after their morning walk.

"You're good for me, girl… in more ways than one. Yes, I love you too," she said accepting Ginger's kisses on her cheek. She laughed, gave her pup a little hug, and turned on the TV. "Let's see what's going on this morning."

There was nothing of great interest on the morning show at that moment, so she grabbed her iPad off the side table. Bonnie had started following Facebook more since Frank died. It was a way of staying connected to her children and friends. Of course, she also talked to them on the phone, even Skyped sometimes, but she loved seeing all the pictures, and it passed the time between her many activities.

She turned her attention back to the TV when she realized they were switching to the local news. She was anxious to hear the weather forecast and learn how much snow she should expect. The reporter stated that the hit-and-run victim from the previous day remained in critical condition. He was identified as a seventy-one-year-old white male who lived on Robin Drive in Madison. This grabbed Bonnie's attention because it was her old neighborhood. Then the announcer said his name—Joseph Marconi. Bonnie sat straight up bringing Ginger to attention.

"Joe! Oh Ginger, it's Joe. I have to go see him."

Joe Marconi was a member of her church and sang in the choir with her. He was also a very good friend and golfing buddy of Frank's. Bonnie thought of how often Joe had visited when Frank was in the hospital. She also remembered his comforting presence after her husband's death. Once her son Mark had gone back home, Joe was one of the men who offered to help her out anytime she needed anything. He'd even offered to come take care of snow removal over the winter, before she decided to sell the house.

Bonnie got Ginger settled in her crate, so glad the pup seemed to like it. Then she put her winter coat back on, added a pair of warm boots, grabbed her keys and gloves and was out the door in record time. She felt a sense of urgency.

The whole drive, Bonnie had to focus on the now snow-covered roads, but her mind kept wandering. *What if I don't get there in time?*

The words 'remains in critical condition' were frightening. *Please God, don't take him today. I don't want to lose anyone else. I pray for your healing touch.* The next words that came into her head were not her own. *"Trust in the Lord."* She breathed more easily then, but was glad to see the hospital come into sight.

When she arrived at Joe's room, she felt a huge flood of relief. At least they had moved him from the ICU to a regular room, and the nurse was an old friend from one of her Bible study groups. She spoke optimistically about his prognosis. There were flowers in the room, and Bonnie wondered who had sent them. *Probably Joe Jr. or his daughter Angela.*

He was sleeping, but the nurse explained he was heavily sedated with pain medication. He had undergone emergency surgery, and come through it well. Now he needed time for his body to heal. Fortunately, there were no internal injuries. At his age the broken bones would take time, but it was the loss of blood that had been the greatest concern.

"Honestly," the nurse told Bonnie, "his vitals are much stronger in the past hour. The doctor hasn't been in yet this morning, but I think he may be over the hump."

It wasn't a very long walk from the halfway house to the hospital, but in the snow and biting cold Susan found it to be quite long enough. She had hesitated to walk the six blocks in such inclement weather, yet felt she had no choice after what she heard on the news. She had to get there, and she had to get there now.

Susan had gone online to learn more about the accident victim. When she heard his name, the world seemed somehow darker and scarier. *Not Joe!* She knew him from the church she used to attend. But he was so much more. He was Marty's uncle, and had been almost like a father to her in many ways.

She hadn't seen Uncle Joe for over a year and didn't expect they would see much of each other at all after she and Marty separated. But now he was lying in the hospital in critical condition because he'd been hit by a car. Hit by someone who didn't stop to get help for him. Someone who left him there to die. *But who?*

Having worked at Madison General for years, Susan knew her way around and knew many of the people working there... doctors, nurses, aides, cafeteria workers, and volunteers. She checked at the information desk then took the elevator to his floor. She had worked in the pediatric wing for a long time before losing her job there, so she didn't know everyone on the surgical ward. She decided to skip the nurses' station and go straight to the room Joe was reported to be in.

When she reached the door, which was ajar, she put one foot inside then quickly backed out. The woman inside hadn't seen or heard her, and that was the way Susan wanted to keep it. She had just glanced Bonnie standing with her purse on her shoulder. Retreating, Susan decided to make herself scarce for the moment. She slipped into the waiting room a few doors down and kept watch until she saw Bonnie leave and head toward the elevator. Then she crept into the room to see for herself how Marty's Uncle Joe was doing.

His face was bruised and swollen, he had a bandage on his head, and his leg was in traction. What scared her the most, though, was his coloring. He looked pasty white... the look of someone who had lost a lot of blood.

"Did I do this to you, Uncle Joe?" Susan whispered. She felt the tears slipping out of the corners of her eyes and swiped them away sniffing.

"Hello!" the voice chirped behind her.

Susan froze. *Did she hear me?*

The nurse came around to the other side of the bed to check the patient's vitals and smiled at Susan. "Are you related to Mr. Marconi?"

"Uh, yes, by marriage. He's my husband's uncle." Susan moved nervously from one foot to the other and avoided eye contact with the young nurse who didn't seem to even take notice. She was busy checking monitors and recording vitals on his chart.

She finally looked up at Susan and smiled. "He seems to be getting stronger each time I've checked him this morning. We're getting lots of positive signs." She looked back at the patient and spoke a little louder.

"Mr. Marconi? Joe? Can you wake up for me?" She made several attempts, but Joe was unresponsive.

Susan's mouth felt dry. "What's wrong?"

"Oh, nothing, ma'am, don't be alarmed. With the pain medications he's on, it's normal for him to be hard to rouse. You can talk to him if you want. He might be awake enough to hear you but too drowsy to open his eyes and respond."

Susan nodded dumbly.

"I'll be back in to check on him in a little while, but ring or come out to the nurses' station if you need anything."

Susan let out her breath when she was alone again. She looked at Joe Marconi lying so still and realized she didn't know what she could possibly say.

Did I do this to you? No! I couldn't have.

She wasn't sure how long she had been standing there, but she struggled to breathe. She had to get out… to get away. She spun around and fled the room. She didn't see Uncle Joe's eyes flutter with an effort to open before he went back into a deeper sleep.

Heading for the exit that was closest to the direction she had to walk, Susan was pulling on her gloves and nearly collided with a woman coming out of the hospital coffee shop.

"Susan! What are you doing here?"

Susan looked up into the eyes of her old friend, Bonnie Dixon.

CHAPTER THIRTY-SEVEN

Sarah slammed the papers down on the island. "Can you believe this?" The look on Craig's face told her he had no idea what she was talking about. "Look at this homework assignment. Seriously? For third grade? That's just not right." Bobby stared open-mouthed at his mother. Seeing his expression, Sarah reined herself in and added calmly, "Sorry kiddo, but you should have shown this to me sooner. I could have helped you."

Craig pushed the assignment back to his wife. "It does look like a little much, but I think he could have handled it." He turned to the child. "Why didn't you finish your homework last night? I saw you working on your model before bed, so you still had time."

Sarah saw Bobby's chin quiver, and she knew what was next. "It's okay, bud. Just go get your things while I write a note to your teacher." She saw Craig tighten his lips. "What?"

"Are you sure you should be making excuses for him?"

"Are you sure you should be telling me how to raise my son?" she snapped. As soon as the words were out of her mouth, she wished she could retrieve them. The other three children hastily made their exits. But Sarah hadn't missed their shocked expressions.

"Wow," Craig said getting to his feet. He circled the island quickly as his wife burst into tears. "It's all right," he assured her.

"I'm sorry. It's these damn hormones," she sobbed. Never before had she spoken of her child with such ownership. And though it was quickly hidden, Sarah had seen the hurt in her husband's eyes. "You know I didn't mean that. I don't even know where it came from."

"I know, I know," Craig soothed. "And you've got a helluva nerve being human just because you're pregnant," he teased. "Forget about it. Now, you have a note to write."

"Okay, but I won't let him off the hook completely." Grabbing the papers, Sarah scribbled, *Bobby felt overwhelmed and did not complete his assignment last night, but I assure you we will have him catch up on unfinished work this weekend before letting him take part in fun activities.* She showed the note to Craig who kissed her on the forehead.

"You're a good mom," he said, "and you'll do as a wife too," he added sliding his hand under her shirt.

"Stop that!" Sarah scolded, looking past him to make sure they weren't being observed by young eyes. Then she looked up through lashes… The look showed her desire to assent to his amorous pleas.

Laughing as he heard the troops heading back to the kitchen for their goodbyes, Craig muttered, "To be continued."

Sarah sighed and closed the client folder before her. She recalled being a grad student and the advice she'd been given by her professor, Bonnie Dixon… *it's important, if you're going to help others, to have your own stuff out of the way.* "That was good advice, my friend," she mumbled. Hearing about the bizarre behavior of her client's husband, Sarah remembered her father's schizophrenia and its tragic consequences that resulted in four deaths including his own. But the man described had begun taking medication and was doing well on it. Sarah felt reassured there would be no murder/suicide in this case. All the same, Sarah had helped her client develop a plan to be safe in any circumstance.

Glancing at the time, Sarah put away the memories of her own father and opened another folder. *Oh, this should be fun,* she thought as she set it aside and went to greet her next client. She had been working with this young woman for nearly six months and thought, at first, she had a very poor prognosis. But Holly had surprised her.

"Hi Sarah," Holly said cheerfully. She took her usual spot in the chair next to the therapist's desk, but she didn't sit back, and she certainly didn't slouch the way she had in their earlier sessions. In fact, she sat perched on the edge of the seat as though about to fly.

After their usual brief greeting, Sarah decided to dig right in. "So, what's going on? You look like a kid at Christmas."

Holly smiled shyly then held out her left hand. The third finger was adorned with a tiny, sparkling diamond ring. "I'm engaged!" she proclaimed.

Sarah's jaw dropped, then her eyes met her client's and read the sheer joy that shone even more than the engagement ring. "Congratulations, sweetie. I'm so happy for you. So, Tim finally popped the question?" She'd known about her client's blossoming love with the young man and even had him come in for a session with Holly a few weeks earlier. "Look at you. Look how far you've come."

Holly smiled, "Thanks to you."

"No, my dear, thanks to you. I just helped you find the inner strength you didn't know you had. You're the one who did all the work. And I congratulate you. Has Tim told his little boy the news?" They had discussed the challenges involved in being a stepmother, but Sarah believed her client was up to the challenge.

Hours later while preparing for bed, Sarah shared her news with Craig. "This was a good day." She pulled back the covers and sat cross-legged facing her husband. "I discharged a client after six months of watching her become totally empowered. It was amazing."

Craig smiled, "That's what it's all about, right?"

"Absolutely. And I really think she's going to do well. She's starting a new chapter in her life," she said. "As I always do, I left the door opened for her to call me if she needs a little help along the way." She hesitated before adding, "She's going to be a stepmother soon so there could be some bumps in the road." Sarah wondered if Craig knew she was thinking about her own careless remark that morning.

His next words told her he did. "But if there's enough love and faith in each other, those little bumps aren't a threat to what they have."

Sarah went willingly as he pulled her down next to him and rested his chin on top of her head. "Craig?"

"Hmm?"

"You know I didn't mean it, right?"

"I know, angel." He slid lower on the pillows and lifted her chin. "I know." Sarah didn't get a chance to say any more as her next words were silenced by his kiss... a kiss that led to what they'd both had on their minds since their early morning flirtation. "Are you purring?" Craig asked with a deep throaty laugh.

"Mmm, maybe," she answered. As their bodies melted into each other, there was no room for questions. There was no room for anything but their growing desire.

Chapter Thirty-Eight

onnie was taken totally by surprise when she ran into Susan at the hospital. She knew Susan didn't work there anymore—hadn't worked there since she had been discovered drinking on the job and then driving while intoxicated. So, seeing her there was confusing.

Susan stammered something about coming to see an old friend, but when Bonnie asked who, Susan was rather vague… something about a friend she had worked with. "I've got to get going," she said, turning to head the far way down the hall.

"But the parking lot and garage are this way." Bonnie gestured toward the opposite end of the corridor.

"Oh, I know. But I walked."

Bonnie remembered Susan had lost her license and immediately felt bad for bringing it up. She couldn't imagine letting her old friend walk in this weather. Since she had dropped her at the halfway house when released from prison, Bonnie knew it would be a rather long walk in the cold.

"Susan, wait!" Bonnie called after her, but thought for a moment she wasn't going to answer. After a couple more steps, though, the younger woman slowly turned back with a questioning look. "Let me give you a ride."

Again, Susan hesitated.

Bonnie couldn't quite read the expression on her face and thought she looked almost frightened. *No wonder, after all she's been through…*

Then, with a sheepish smile, Susan came back toward her. "Thanks, Bonnie. It is pretty miserable out there. I appreciate it."

"No problem. It's not at all out of the way."

The two women walked in awkward silence. The kind of uncomfortable silence between two people who feel like they should say

151

something but can't find the words. It wasn't until they had reached the car that either of them spoke.

"Did you hear about the hit-and-run accident the other night?" Bonnie asked her passenger. She thought Susan jumped like a scared rabbit. Then, when Susan confirmed, she added, "Do you remember Joseph Marconi from church? He was in the choir with me? Remember?"

Susan didn't answer right away. Her face had gone ashen.

"Are you all right, dear?"

"Ye… yes, I… I hadn't heard who it was." Then she turned to face Bonnie and continued. "Joe Marconi is Marty's uncle."

"Oh, I'm so sorry. I think I did know that, but I had completely forgotten." *No wonder she looked so shocked.* "I wonder if Marty has heard about it."

Susan was looking straight ahead through the windshield.

"Oh, I'm so sorry. I didn't mean to upset you. I probably shouldn't have asked you that. I didn't mean to make you uncomfortable. I seem to be handling this all wrong."

"No, it's okay, Bonnie. Don't worry about it."

They rode the rest of the way in silence. When Bonnie pulled up to the halfway house, it seemed Susan couldn't get out fast enough. She stuck her head back in long enough to thank Bonnie for the ride, slammed the car door, and headed inside.

Bonnie watched until the door closed behind her then pulled away from the curb with an uneasy feeling. That feeling followed her all the way back to her cottage, and she shared her confusion with Ginger when she got there. Ginger, however, gave her no answers—just lots and lots of kisses.

"Well you're no help at all!" Bonnie laughed. She dug her cell phone out of her purse, opened to her recent calls and hit Val's number. "Hello there, my friend. How are you?"

Val shared that schools had announced a two-hour delay, and then wound up closing for the day. There was no sign of the snow letting up, and the latest forecast called for five to six inches.

"It looks beautiful, but it certainly does put a cramp in my plans," Bonnie complained.

"Oh, is this your book club day?"

"No, actually I figured Ginger and I would curl up with a good book and a pot of tea. But then I heard something on the news that changed everything. Did you hear about Joe?"

Val had turned the TV off after catching a weather update, so Bonnie filled her in.

"Oh Bonnie, that's just horrible. And I know he and Frank were such good friends."

Bonnie swallowed the lump in her throat and blinked back tears. "I went over to Madison General to see him this morning."

"In this weather? Bonnie, should you be driving?"

"No, probably not, but I had to see him, and it wasn't all that bad when I left. It was quite a bit worse coming back home, but I have four-wheel drive, and I took my time, so I didn't have any problems."

Val asked how Joe was doing, and Bonnie told her as much as she knew which wasn't a whole lot.

"And then you'll never guess who I ran into—Susan Walters."

Val didn't respond immediately. After a thoughtful pause, she asked "Why… and was she sober?"

"As far as I could see. But then she did have a bandage on her forehead like she'd taken a fall." Bonnie frowned. "I tried talking to Ginger about it, but she was no help at all." She heard Val laughing on the other end of the line. "Honestly, I love the little fur-ball, but she's not very helpful with something like this. If it weren't for this weather, you would have had a visitor for lunch."

Bonnie smiled, picturing her friend pushing away from the desk in her home office and rocking back in her chair. "I don't know why exactly, but I've been uneasy ever since I talked to Susan."

Bonnie told Val about Susan's reaction when she heard Joe Marconi was the victim of the hit-and-run driver.

"Did you know Joe was Marty Walters' uncle?"

Val gasped.

"Yeah, small world." Bonnie went on to explain how she happened to be driving Susan home. "And it was a rather awkward ride. I seem to always have my foot in my mouth with that woman. I certainly don't mean to upset her, but I don't know, she just seems overly sensitive and very strange," Bonnie sighed, "even without the alcohol."

CHAPTER THIRTY-NINE

Susan didn't want to think about it, but she had no choice. She followed the news every day, many times a day, always fearful… so afraid of what the ongoing police investigation would discover. She had never found the rental car and had no idea where she could have left it… and how she'd gotten to the park again without it. Maybe the rental company had found it wherever she left it. She didn't think they could track it back to her since she'd used that phony ID. But the rental company didn't find the car. The police did.

Susan quickly skimmed the update then went back and read it again. It said they found the car that hospitalized Marconi. It had been abandoned miles from town in a lot of underbrush. They gave no further details as it was a continuing investigation.

Susan felt sick. She wiped her sweaty hand on her jeans and stared at the computer screen. *But that's at least a mile from the park. Did I walk all the way back from there?*

"Are you all right, Susan?"

It was Nancy. It seemed to Susan that every time she turned around, Nancy was there, watching her… asking if she was okay.

"I'm fine. No, I'm not fine." She knew Nancy wasn't buying the 'I'm fine' line so she decided to give her a reason. "I miss my little girl!"

"Of course you do. When do you get to see her again? This weekend?"

"Yeah, for a couple of hours. Big whoop. Then I have to say goodbye again." Susan was still bitter in spite of everything.

"You know you can have her back with you once you've established you're ready, right?"

"Yes, I know." Susan did know that, but what Nancy didn't know was she might be going back to prison. *If Joe dies, my life will be over, too.* In utter desolation, her tears began to fall again. She was shaken to her very core by the thought of what she must have done.

She was startled by Nancy's sudden embrace. "You can do this, Susan. Let me help you."

Susan was touched by the kindness, but she didn't see how Nancy could possibly help. How could anyone help her? But she returned Nancy's embrace. Feeling so totally alone and hopeless, she needed this. She needed to know someone cared… even if it wouldn't last. *How can anyone care about me?*

♥

Susan stood at the front door of Val and Andy's house. She hated coming to this place—having to face Val, knowing how much the woman must hate her for what she'd done. *How could I ever expect her to forgive me? I cheated with her husband. I had his little girl, and then I even messed that up.*

The door opened almost immediately after she rang the bell. She didn't see Elizabeth right away, and was suddenly afraid her daughter might not want to see her. Elizabeth had been so hesitant the last time. But then she saw her approaching with a big smile on her face. It seemed the fear had disappeared.

"Momma!" Elizabeth ran into her arms, and Susan saw Val step back.

"Susan, would you like a cup of coffee or tea? I put some snacks in the family room for you two to enjoy while you visit."

"Oh, thanks, and no, nothing to drink… or maybe just some water?" Susan really wanted something a little stronger, but she hadn't had a drink since her blackout. She was afraid what might happen if she dared to sneak one. Afraid she wouldn't stop.

"Oh, my sweet Elizabeth, you're getting so big."

Elizabeth smiled proudly. "I'm six now. I had a birthday!"

Susan opened her eyes wide, as if in surprise. "Oh my goodness!" she said thinking, *and I wasn't here.* "You are, aren't you? But you're still my baby!" Susan squeezed her giggling little girl as tightly as she dared, and when she finally loosened her grip, Elizabeth led her to the family room where there was a small platter of sandwiches with the crusts cut off.

Val brought in a pitcher of ice water and a glass she'd already poured. After Susan thanked her, she discreetly disappeared into the kitchen.

Elizabeth offered her mother a sandwich pushing the platter toward her, and Susan noticed there were several peanut butter and jelly and a couple of ham and cheese for the more grown-up taste. Elizabeth took a bite of her sandwich then popped up out of her seat and grabbed a folder off one of the side tables.

"Wanna look at my papers from conferences?" she asked. *Conferences?* Susan thought. *Parent-Teacher conferences—but who went with you, Elizabeth?*

"Sure princess, of course... I want to see everything!" Elizabeth showed off samples of her writing, which Susan thought had really improved.

The child chatted so comfortably Susan began to relax. But at the same time, she had a nagging miserable memory of all the times Elizabeth had wanted to talk about what happened at school, but her mother had been too foggy to pay attention or care.

The rest of their visit passed uneventfully, but when it was time to go, Susan's heart was broken.

"Momma, don't go... please don't go!" Elizabeth was crying and hanging onto her neck.

Susan was relieved to know her daughter still wanted her in her life, but was horrified she had to hurt her yet again.

Val stood behind them, waiting. Susan looked up, expecting to see scorn or judgment, or anything but what she saw. What she read on Val's face was compassion. Val actually looked like she was hurting, too.

Well, of course. She's feeling bad for Elizabeth, not me!

Susan couldn't believe Val could feel anything but hatred toward her. She finally managed to peel her child's arms from around her, and with tears falling from her own eyes, backed out of the house and pulled the door closed behind her. She caught her breath and made a dash to the taxi waiting at the curb, but as the driver pulled away, she took one last glance up at the house.

There in the picture window she saw her child, her heartbroken Elizabeth, tears still flowing, in the arms of another woman. *I'll be back Elizabeth... I promise!*

CHAPTER FORTY

"Andy, you should have seen her. It was just awful!" Val sat on the side of the bed massaging lavender-scented cream onto her hands. Andy reached up and rubbed her back.

"I know, sweetheart. Betsy has been through way too much for a little girl her age."

Val spun and looked at her husband. "No! I mean Susan!"

"What?" Now Andy was the one who seemed puzzled.

"Well, I mean, of course it was awful for Betsy too, but if you could have seen Susan's face... it broke my heart. I think about Craig when he was that age, and I can't even imagine..."

Andy didn't respond right away, but Val saw something on his face that concerned her. "What are you thinking, Andy?" Still, he hesitated. "What?" Val asked in exasperation.

"Well, it's just that... I've been thinking, well, I *am* Betsy's father. And I've seen the way you are with her. I mean, you really seem to care about her."

"Of course I care about her!" Val snapped. "What are you getting at?" She wasn't sure exactly what she expected, but the sense of dread sat like a lump in her chest.

"Okay, don't get mad... I mean think about it for a minute... I've just been wondering if she would be better off here... with us... I mean permanently."

Val's eyebrows shot up and her jaw dropped. He had to be kidding. She leaped up from the bed and started pacing around the bedroom. "Are you kidding? I mean seriously, Andy?" He tried to interrupt, but she cut him off. "Look, no, you listen to me. Susan is her mother! Yes, I care about Betsy... I more than care about her. I've come to love that little girl, but no... no way. You can't even think about taking her away from her mother." Val's voice had grown louder with her vehement objections.

"Shhh, Val, don't wake her! Listen, I'm sorry. I just thought…"

Val saw how miserable he looked and regretted her impassioned response. "I know, dear… or maybe I don't know," Val said apologetically. "I can't imagine what you're feeling. But, well, I'm a mother. As much as I've tried to stay angry with Susan—and God knows I have resented her—I can't imagine what that would do to her. We can't take her child away."

"We didn't intend to take her in the first place," Andy said. "She's the one who created this situation. If she hadn't put my daughter's life in jeopardy and called me to rescue her, it never would have crossed my mind."

Val heard the anger in his voice and knew it was justified. How could she argue the point? But she knew she had to try. "Andy, listen…" She was interrupted by the sound of crying. "Oh God, do you think she heard us?" Val headed for the door, but Andy stopped her.

"Let me," he said as he passed her and headed down the hall.

Val fell back onto the bed feeling tired, confused, scared, and utterly frustrated.

♥

When Andy came back to the master suite, Val thought he looked completely defeated. He had been gone for quite a while.

"Is she okay? Did she hear us?"

"No," Andy sighed. "She had another bad dream. She was really upset, even though she was still half asleep."

"Was she able to tell you what the dream was about this time?" Val had comforted Betsy more than once when she woke up from a nightmare, but the poor girl never seemed to remember what scared her.

"Yes, well, bits and pieces." Andy turned to face his wife. She saw the agony in his eyes. "She told me about the one part that was clear. The ground was splitting apart, and her mother was on the other side of the opening which kept getting bigger. She said her momma was getting farther and farther away, and couldn't get to her." Andy rubbed his hand back and forth across his forehead. "When she was trying to tell me about it, she started crying again."

"Is she all right now? Is there anything I can do?"

"No, she's back to sleep. I held her until she started breathing evenly, then laid her back down on the pillow. She seems to be sleeping peacefully now."

Val saw his chin quiver and he took a deep breath and blew it out slowly.

"I guess you were right, Val. Betsy belongs with her momma."

CHAPTER FORTY-ONE

Susan's time with her daughter in the afternoon had been the final motivation she needed to push her into recovery. Her priorities were now crystal clear.

No matter how difficult, she had to stay sober.

When she got back to the halfway house she checked the kitchen, the big living room where they relaxed during their free time, and the little library/computer room. Then she went straight to Nancy's room and knocked on the door.

"Come on in," Nancy called from inside.

Susan opened the door and immediately started talking. The words spilled out in a rush. She had to talk fast before she lost her nerve. "Nancy, I need your help. You said you were here for me if I needed you... and I do." Tears came unbidden. "Please, I can't do this alone... please can you help me?"

Before the last words were out of her mouth, Nancy's arms were around her, and Susan found herself crying on her new friend's shoulder—like a child being comforted by her mother—comfort she'd never gotten from her own mother.

Nancy was a counselor in the halfway house, but she was also a recovering alcoholic with fourteen years clean. She knew the signs, and she undoubtedly knew Susan was struggling and had probably had a slip. "Susan, it's okay. Whatever is wrong, we'll get you through it. You are stronger than you know." As Susan's tears subsided, Nancy led her to one of the two comfortable chairs in her room, and pulled the other one up close. "Now tell me. What's going on?"

Susan described the scene at the end of her visit with Elizabeth. "I have to do better. I have to be a better mother to my little girl. She deserves better. I'm afraid I'm going to lose her for good, Nancy. Oh God, I just can't lose her."

"We just take it one day at a time… and you *will* get your child back. I promise you, if you stick with the program, if you listen to your heart… and your sponsor… you will have Elizabeth with you." She held Susan at arm's length, looked into her eyes, and added, "It will happen when you're ready. And when it's safe for both of you."

Susan had had a sponsor assigned to her while she was incarcerated, but since she was only pretending then, she hadn't really listened to much of anything she'd been told. Now she looked at Nancy. "I know this is going to sound stupid of me, but I don't really have anyone… a sponsor, I mean."

"Well, what about me? Would you like me to be your sponsor?"

"Are you serious? Would you do that?"

"Of course. What step are you on?"

Susan thought about that for a while and decided this was no time for lies and deceit. It was truth time. "To be honest, Nancy, I've just been going through the motions. I think I need to start back at the first step. I mean, if that's okay. I said and wrote what was expected," Susan stared at the floor remembering the message of step one, "but until the last couple of days I guess I never accepted I was powerless over alcohol. I can see now, my life has become unmanageable. I'm kind of a slow learner, huh?" She looked up and read understanding in Nancy's smile.

"It takes most of us a long time to learn that lesson, but to answer your question, yes, that's definitely a good idea. I think that's the best decision to get you on the real road to recovery."

♥

"Hi, my name is Susan, and I'm an alcoholic." This was the first time Susan had said those words and acknowledged the truth in them. She blinked back tears as the other women in the room said, "Hi, Susan." The next words would be even harder. She looked across the room at her sponsor who had come to the meeting with her. Nancy smiled and gave her a slight nod.

"I have been sober for one week."

She saw Penny's jaw drop and then quickly close as she tried not to show her surprise. Susan smiled sheepishly, but the smile faded as she continued to share.

The most difficult part to talk about was the night she had the accident with Elizabeth in the car. "And I would never have forgiven myself if anything had happened to my daughter. She is the most important person in the world to me and the reason I realized I had to stop lying to myself and take my life back." Susan accepted the tissue Penny handed her and swiped at the tears now streaming down her face. "And I pray one of these days I will earn the right to have her back with me." She looked at Nancy again and added, "But only when I know it's safe."

After the meeting, Susan socialized briefly, amazed at how accepting everyone seemed to be in spite of the fact she'd confessed to drinking just one week earlier. It felt good. But still, in the back of her mind, she knew there was a lie.

I can't tell them that part, Susan thought. *If the truth about that night ever comes out, I could lose my daughter forever.*

Back in her room, Susan opened the journal Nancy had given her after they talked. She spent the next hour writing from her heart. When she put down her pen, she felt completely drained but with a fresh sense of relief. She was already in her pajamas but had to brush her teeth. *I'm going to rot my teeth with all this candy.* The candy seemed to help a little though, so she decided to take extra good care with brushing and flossing.

When she was finally ready for bed, she lay staring at the ceiling wondering what kind of job Nancy had in mind when she said she would help her with her employment search tomorrow. She didn't think about it too long though. For the first night in a very long time—pushing that one dark secret out of her mind—Susan drifted quickly into a peaceful sleep.

Chapter Forty-Two

The next morning Susan went online and checked the local news station's update on the hit-and-run story. Marconi's status had been upgraded to fair. She let out her breath. *Thank God, he's not going to die.*

The article went on to say the investigation into the circumstances of the accident was ongoing. *Uncle Joe is conscious. I should go see him. Or should I?* She wondered if he had seen anything. She wondered if he'd seen her that night. Most of all, she wondered if she was going back to jail.

Since she had finished her morning chores and wouldn't be meeting with Nancy until the afternoon, Susan decided to take a walk. It was still pretty cold, but there was no wind today, and no precipitation. She grabbed her coat and gloves and headed out the door. There was no conscious decision to go to the hospital, but that's where she found herself.

What are you doing, Susan?

The warning went unheeded. She was drawn into the corridor and up the elevator to Uncle Joe's room as if it was a magnet and she was made of iron.

But she didn't feel like she was made of iron. Her legs felt more like rubber. She stood outside his door searching for the courage to enter and had nearly changed her mind, when the same perky nurse she'd run into before, appeared at the door.

"Oh, hi there! Mr. Marconi is awake. You can go right in."

Susan thanked her and inched her way into the room. The bed had been partially raised, and Susan saw immediately that Marty's uncle was very much improved. She had taken several steps into the room before he noticed her.

He looked puzzled at first, then she saw the light of recognition in his eyes, and held her breath. His face gradually brightened with the smile she remembered.

"Is that my little Sue?" His voice was weak but clear. "Come in, come on in. Let me look at you."

Susan walked to the side of his bed. He reached out his hand, and she took it in hers. "How are you doing, Uncle Joe?"

"Oh, I'm good, darlin'. You can't keep an old bird like me down. But look at you! How long has it been?"

Susan wasn't sure but knew it was more than a year.

"Does an old man have to get hit by a car to get a visit?" he winked.

"I'm sorry, Uncle Joe. I… I haven't had a chance… I mean…"

"Never mind. It's okay. I know you've been having some problems. Marty told me all about it."

Susan felt her face flush. Why hadn't she realized Marty would have told him all about what she'd done? Now she couldn't look at the old man.

"Hey, Sue, I said it's okay. Just because you and Marty have your problems doesn't make me love you any less… or that little girl either."

Susan wondered how much Marty had told his uncle. Maybe he didn't know all the gruesome details. "Well, I know you're Marty's uncle and all, but I wanted to come see for myself how you were doing." Susan sat in the chair by the bed and glanced up at the TV where an old western was on. The sound was turned down too low to hear. Susan wondered why it was even on.

"Sue, are you okay, darlin'?"

She looked down at the floor.

"I don't mean to pry or make you feel uncomfortable…"

Susan could literally hear him tiring and knew she shouldn't stay too long. "No, hush, Uncle Joe. You're not prying, but I don't want you to tire yourself out. I'm just so glad you're okay." She didn't mean to cry, but there it was.

He patted her hand, and she knew he had no idea how relieved she was that he had survived.

"Now don't you worry, Sue, no stupid drunk is going to be the death of me!" He laughed as he said it, but she read more than just humor in his words. "Can you believe that bastard just left me lying there in the street? That's all right. He'll pay. Either here... or there." He raised his eyes as he said the last word.

Susan felt the hairs on the back of her neck stand on end. She suddenly felt hot and clammy. She had to get out of there. Getting to her feet, she told Joe again how glad she was that he was getting better. She gave him a quick peck on the forehead and promised to come and visit again soon.

"Oh, they're not going to keep me here much longer. A man can't live on this hospital food." He laughed weakly and relaxed into his pillow.

Susan glanced back as she got to the door, and saw his eyes were closed.

Back outside, she breathed deeply and waited for the cold air to revive her. *God, I need a drink. No! That's not the answer.* She shook her head, then headed back to the house. It was almost lunchtime, and she felt her stomach growling. It was time to start taking better care of herself.

When she got within a half block of the halfway house, Susan stopped. She crossed the street to the other side and kept walking. Her mind raced. Her chest tightened. She rushed away from the black and white threat. *Oh God, it's the police.*

Susan quickened her pace. She walked to the corner, took a right, went to the next corner, took another right, and kept going for several blocks. The cold bit into her toes. *Susan Walters, you're a fool. You can't just walk around all day.*

Her feet went from ice to lead as she finally approached the corner of her street, but when she turned down the block she breathed a huge sigh of relief. The police car was gone.

Susan hurried—almost running the rest of the way—anxious to get warm, and was relieved no one greeted her at the door. She went straight to her room and tossed her coat on the bed, but she had no sooner flopped into a chair than there was a knock on the door.

She froze. There was another knock.

"Susan... it's me... Nancy."

Susan took a deep breath and put on her best poker-face. "Come on in, Nancy." She gave her biggest smile. "It's not time for our meeting yet, is it?" She reached for her phone to check the time, knowing the meeting with her sponsor was still an hour away.

"No, I just wanted to tell you something."

Susan raised her eyebrows with interest, while her insides shook in dread of what Nancy's next words might be. And she was right.

"A police officer was here looking for you and left just a few minutes before you got back. Do you know what it's all about?"

Susan did her best to mask her fear with a look of curiosity. "No, didn't he say?"

"It was a female officer actually, but no, she didn't. Oh, but she gave me her card, and said to have you call her." Nancy handed Susan the card, and Susan tried not to let her hand shake as she accepted it.

"Hmm, okay, thanks." She looked at the card, put it on the side table, and smiled up at Nancy. "So, I'll see you shortly, and I'll bring my journal, okay?" She thought Nancy looked a little perplexed, but agreed. It wasn't until the door closed behind her that Susan let out her breath. She picked up the card and stared at it. Shakily returning it to the table, she turned to look out the window.

Somewhere out there people were living their normal lives. They went to work, came home, sat around the dinner table with their families, and relaxed in front of the TV. They weren't living in halfway houses or prisons. They weren't drunks who did terrible things... like hitting a man with their car and leaving him to die. And they weren't afraid to answer a call from a police officer who probably knew what they'd done.

She was pulled back to her reality by the ringing of her cell phone. Susan jumped at the sound and wiped away the tears that streaked her makeup. After a moment's hesitation, she checked the caller ID. She didn't know the number, but it wasn't the same as the one on the card. When it rang for the fourth time, she bit her lower lip, snatched up the phone, and accepted the call.

"Hello?" It was barely more than a whisper.

"Hi, Susan?" The voice sounded familiar, but Susan couldn't quite place it.

"Yes, this is she. Who's this?" she asked nervously.

"This is Valerie Reed."

Susan breathed more easily for the second before panic struck her. "Is something wrong with Elizabeth? Is she okay?"

"Oh, she's fine, Susan. I'm sorry. I didn't mean to scare you."

Well you certainly did!

"It's just that B— I mean Elizabeth has really been missing you, and she keeps asking when she can see you again… So, well, Andy and I just wondered if you might want to come join us for dinner."

Susan was dumbfounded. She was so completely caught off-guard she couldn't think what to say.

"We would understand if you'd rather not," Val hastened to add. "I mean I didn't want to put you in an uncomfortable position, so I didn't tell Elizabeth we were going to invite you. I won't say anything to her if—"

"No, please, I mean, thank you. But are you sure? I mean…"

"Yes, I'm sure. And Andy is fine with it, too. I know we all just want what's best for your daughter."

When Susan ended the call, she sat in a state of shock. She couldn't believe Val had actually invited her to have a meal with them—to sit in their house, at their table, with them.

They had been friends once, but that seemed like a lifetime ago. *Is it possible? Could we actually be friends again someday?* She dismissed the thought quickly as ludicrous. It was like Val said, they just wanted to do what was best for Elizabeth.

Suddenly none of that mattered. All that mattered was she was going to see her little girl in a few hours. She went to the closet and looked at the few clothes she had there. She chose something simple in sapphire blue—Elizabeth loved blue—and laid the clothes out so she could get dressed as soon as her meeting with Nancy ended.

As she turned to pick up her phone and check the time, Susan's eyes rested on Officer Tomlin's card. *No, not now!*

Susan was surprised that she was able to completely put everything aside during her time with Nancy. Their focus was on the first of the twelve steps of the program, and she gave it every bit of her concentration.

But it all came crashing back into her brain the moment they finished talking about the step and Nancy asked if she'd gotten in touch with the officer who left her card.

"No, I didn't reach her yet, and I really have to get going." Susan quickly changed the subject. "Oh, guess what… I get to see Elizabeth tonight."

Nancy looked surprised.

"Yeah, the Reeds invited me to dinner with them."

"Wow, that's kind of unexpected, isn't it?" Nancy didn't know all the details, but Susan had explained that the relationship between herself and the Reeds was strained, to say the least.

"Yes," Susan agreed, "it was totally unexpected, but Val said Elizabeth has been asking when she could see me again, and they thought it would be good for her."

"Wow! Well that's great. Enjoy your time with her, and if you need to talk when you get back, let me know, okay?"

Susan appreciated Nancy's support and agreed, but she was glad to get away from her before she asked anymore about the police. She was also anxious to leave the house in case they returned. Right now, she just wanted to focus on spending this time, these precious moments—that could be the last—with her daughter.

Chapter Forty-Three

Val paced nervously back and forth sneaking peeks out at the street. She had offered to pick Susan up but was actually relieved when she'd declined. Val wondered if she was going to take a taxi or uber or public transportation… or maybe she would get a ride with someone else.

"Aunt Val, why are there four plates on the table, and what smells so good?"

Val hadn't heard Betsy come out of her bedroom and wasn't sure if she should say anything or not. *What if Susan doesn't show up?* But she didn't have to answer. Andy had come in right behind her and heard the question. He grabbed her around the waist and tossed her up in the air. Val was amazed by how agile he still was at the age of fifty-five.

"That wonderful smell is one of your favorites—meatloaf—and that fourth plate is for a surprise we have for you." Andy was grinning from ear to ear.

"What's the surprise? Tell me!" They were interrupted by a knock at the door.

"Well, guess what?" Andy said to her, "I think the surprise is here."

Elizabeth went running to the door right behind Val. With a squeal of delight, she ran into her mother's arms nearly knocking her down as Val pushed the door closed against the wind.

After several minutes of excited back and forth between mother and daughter, Susan looked at Val and Andy who were standing side by side watching them. "Thank you," Susan mouthed. Val smiled and nodded. It felt good to see Betsy so happy. Val looked up at her husband and saw he was pleased, too. But still, it was odd to watch him smiling at his child and her mother.

It wasn't easy, but she had to push away the jealousy. As if he'd read her mind, Andy put his arm around her and pulled her tight. He gave her a reassuring smile and whispered, "I love you."

Val's shoulders eased down away from her ears as she felt some of the tension drain. She knew he meant it.

It wasn't the most comfortable 'dinner party' Val had ever given, but it may have been the most heart-warming. The difference in Betsy was astounding. Normally the girl would take part in their conversation and answer questions about what she was learning in school and how she was getting along with her friends, but her level of enthusiasm didn't compare to what Val was seeing tonight.

Betsy was like a bundle of endless energy with a million and one things to talk about. Both Val and Susan had urged her to remember to eat, but eating was not the child's top priority this evening. It wasn't until dessert that she even began to slow down. It helped that Val served her very favorite—rocky road ice cream with whipped cream.

There had been very little conversation between the adults as they all focused on Betsy, but there had been many looks. What Val was most aware of were the looks of appreciation from her husband. She saw the same appreciation on Susan's face and had to admit it warmed her heart to see the woman back with her daughter. Susan was obviously sober and that was also reassuring. And her hands weren't even shaky. She was still quite thin, but looked a little better each visit.

By the time the four of them settled in the family room, Betsy was already looking sleepy. It had been a long, eventful day, and Val thought all the excitement had worn her out early.

"I guess I should be going," Susan said, but Val could see she was having trouble tearing herself away from her child.

Betsy crawled onto Susan's lap on the couch and wrapped her arms around her mother's neck. Val looked at Andy, then over at Susan. "It looks like your little girl is getting sleepy. Maybe you could tuck her in before you leave?"

Susan looked up hopefully. "Really?" she asked. "Would you like that, Elizabeth?"

"Yes... and will you read me a story... please?"

Val nodded at Susan's questioning look, and Susan carried her much too heavy little girl to her bedroom.

When they were gone, Val sighed and looked over at her husband who was wearing an expression she couldn't quite read. "What is it, Andy?"

"You're an amazing woman, you know that?" he whispered.

Val saw the love she felt for Andy reflected in his eyes. "It was the right thing to do… for B—I mean Elizabeth… and for Susan," Val added.

♥

Val drove Susan back to the halfway house When she found out she had planned to take public transportation home, Val had objected. "You shouldn't be walking all that way alone at night." The bus stop was at least half a mile away from their house. "Please let me drive you."

She thought Susan was going to refuse at first, but after looking out at the dark, her former friend finally accepted. Val expected it to be an uncomfortable drive, and it was awkward at first with neither of them speaking for several minutes.

But Susan finally broke the silence. "I don't know how to thank you for tonight. I doubt if you can even begin to imagine how much it meant to me to spend this time with my daughter."

Val smiled. "I'm a mother, too. I know this must be horrible for you."

"Yes, but I did it to myself." Susan dropped her eyes. "And to her."

Val was surprised by this admission, but couldn't think of anything to say in response. It was true, after all.

"But Val, I've changed. I mean I'm changing. I'm not going to be that person anymore. I'm going to be the mother Elizabeth deserves… if I get the chance."

Val glanced at her passenger and saw the torment on her face. Susan's last five words had barely been above a whisper. *Whatever does she mean by that?*

Chapter Forty-Four

Susan's stomach churned when she looked up at her temporary home. The brown building looked quite sober itself, even in daylight. Wrapped in the gloomy darkness of a moonless night, it was downright foreboding and filled her with dread. Susan silently prayed nothing had changed since she left.

Val pulled up out front and was waiting expectantly. "Is everything okay, Susan?"

"Yes, yes, and thanks again for tonight and for the ride," she answered awkwardly. Seeing nothing out of the ordinary, she stepped out of the car, and jogged up the front steps. She noticed that Val waited until she opened the door and was safely inside before pulling away. *What a strange day this has been.*

Fortunately, it was only 8:30. She'd could still make it to the late AA meeting which was in the building next door tonight. Although a meeting every day for the first thirty days was all that was mandatory at the halfway house, Nancy had stressed how important it was to attend a meeting every day for the first ninety days now that she had committed to the program. And Susan was determined to do whatever it took to turn her life around.

She slipped quietly into the meeting space and looked around at the mostly familiar faces. There were about ten women in attendance tonight. Most were fellow residents of the halfway house who also attended a meeting every night—or morning or afternoon, depending on the day of the week—while a few others were from the community.

As Susan looked from face to face, she made eye contact with someone she didn't recall seeing before, yet who looked undeniably familiar. *Where have I seen her before?* She thought she saw recognition in the other woman's eyes before she looked away. Susan tried to clear her mind and focus on the speaker. Penny was sharing again, and Susan felt an empathy she hadn't in previous meetings.

177

Moments later Penny took a seat and Nancy, who was running tonight's meeting, asked if anyone else would like to share. The young woman who had caught her eye volunteered to go next. Susan's curiosity was piqued.

"Hi, my name is Janice, and I'm an alcoholic."

Janice! Of course... Susan saw Janice glance at her so she closed her mouth which had dropped open. Now she knew why the woman had looked so familiar. Janice worked at Madison General as a nursing assistant. They hadn't worked closely, but Susan had seen her nearly every day. Somehow, in this setting, she hadn't recognized her.

Susan listened to what Janice was saying, understood her pain, and cheered for the fact that she was celebrating three years of sobriety.

After the group joined in the Serenity Prayer, Susan saw Janice coming toward her.

"How are you? Do you remember me?"

Susan explained that she hadn't recognized her at first but it came to her as soon as she said her name. "But I didn't know..."

"No," Janice said, "not many people at the hospital know I'm an alcoholic."

Susan was surprised at how easily the woman said those words.

"It's not something we advertise, is it?"

"No," Susan laughed, "I guess not. So, I don't mean to pry, but were you working at the hospital when you—"

"When I was drinking?" Janice cut her off. "No, I've only been at the hospital for two years. I actually just moved to Madison about two years ago. I had to get away from the town I'd lived in, the guy I was living with, who was also a drunk, and all the people who were either my old drinking buddies or people who judged me." Janice looked up and smiled, "So, I moved here to Madison to get a fresh start."

"Wow, that took guts."

Back in her room, Susan thought about what Janice had said. She wondered if she would have to move to another town to get a fresh start. *But I don't think they'll let me leave—especially if...*

♥

Sitting by the window, Susan felt the morning sun. It looked like it was finally going to be a nice day. She turned the business card over and over in her hand like a dealer in the casino. To call or not to call. *Do I really have a choice?* She knew if she didn't call eventually they would come for her. In fact, she was surprised they hadn't already shown up at the front door.

That was when the police car pulled up. There were no lights or sirens... just a black and white vehicle with an officer getting out of the driver's side. Susan's stomach flipped and she struggled to breathe... fear grabbed her by the throat... Then she grabbed the phone and quickly dialed the number. She stepped back away from the window, but could still see the officer below stop on the sidewalk and look at her phone.

She stopped walking and answered. "Hello, Officer Tomlin."

"Hi, Officer Tomlin, this is Susan Walters." She was trying hard not to let the officer hear the quiver in her voice, but she couldn't stop shaking. "I got a message that you wanted me to call you."

"Yes, Mrs. Walters, where are you now?"

"I'm at home—I mean at the halfway house where I'm staying right now."

"Oh good," Susan heard what sounded like a little laugh. "I'm right out front. Is it okay if I come in and see you for a few minutes? It won't take long."

"Oh, of course, I'll be right down." Susan ended the call. She wanted to run out the back door. She wanted to run with every fiber of her being... but she couldn't.

She was surprised by the friendly smile on Officer Tomlin's face when she opened the door to her. "Come in." She led her to the living area, which was usually deserted at this hour of the morning. "What is this about, Officer?" She sat down, afraid her legs were about to give out, and Officer Tomlin followed her lead.

"Is it true that on the night of January twenty-ninth you were struck on the head by an unknown assailant?"

Susan felt light-headed as she acknowledged that she was.

"Well, I think I have something that belongs to you. Is it also true you were robbed that night?"

When Susan nodded, the officer continued, "Can you describe what was taken from you."

"Yes, my wallet was stolen. It was blue… and it had some money in it… not a lot… and—"

"That's good enough, Mrs. Walters." She smiled broadly. "We have your wallet down at the station. You just have to go down and fill out a form to pick it up."

"But how? I mean, where did you find it?" Susan's mouth was dry and the world was spinning.

"Well I'm not at liberty to give the details, but it will probably be on the evening news. It was in a car—oh, minus the cash, I'm afraid—that was involved in an accident that night."

Oh my God… they found the car!

CHAPTER FORTY-FIVE

Bonnie looked around the living room of her cottage for the third time in five minutes. Everything seemed to be in order, but she wanted to be sure. This would be the first time her bridge group was coming to her new place. It was quite a change from the big house she and Frank had shared for forty years… where they had raised three children, and where they had made so many memories.

Through the years, Bonnie had made a beautiful home, one she was proud of. Now she had let go of so many of the things that added to its warmth and charm. She sent many pieces of furniture and travel treasures home with her son and two daughters. She'd also donated some things to the Salvation Army and Purple Heart. But as her eyes perused the room, Bonnie knew she had kept enough of the special décor for this to still feel like home. When the doorbell rang, she was satisfied that it was good.

"Val, Sarah, come in. Let me take your coats."

Amidst the shared hugs, Sarah told her not to close the door.

"Kathy pulled in right behind us," Val said.

Within ten minutes, the ladies had their drinks and were seated around the table ready to get the game started. Bonnie bid one heart. Sarah jumped to three clubs, and Val went right to five hearts. Pass. Pass. Pass. Val got the contract, and Bonnie sat out as Dummy. She watched her partner's excellent play and knew Val kept track of every card. She had become quite proficient, and Bonnie enjoyed watching her complete the contract. Her mind wandered back to a time when Val's exhaustion and lack of concentration had made it difficult for her to focus on the game. But it was no wonder.

When she thought about Val's husband and Susan—one of their past bridge group players and a friend—having an affair, Bonnie thought it was a wonder Val had managed to function at all. But now, she appeared to have regained her confidence. Bonnie looked at her friend and thought she could see a change in her just in the past week. Somehow, she seemed more relaxed.

The deal passed to Kathy, who had the habit of shuffling the cards endlessly, so with a break in the action there was time for a little chatter. "So, Val, how did the visit go last night?" Sarah asked.

Bonnie usually knew everything going on in her best friend's life, but she wasn't aware of any special visitor.

"Surprisingly well, actually," Val answered. Bonnie threw her a questioning look so she went on to explain, "Betsy had been really missing her mother since their last visitation, and then she had this horrible nightmare about a chasm in the earth with her on one side and her mother on the other. It was awful. She cried and cried... So anyhow, Andy and I talked about it and thought she really needed to see Susan before next Saturday. So, we called and invited her to dinner."

Bonnie's eyes widened with surprise and Kathy's jaw dropped. Bonnie looked at her friend with admiration. She knew Val had a big heart, and the fact that she had forgiven her husband for being unfaithful had been a testament to that. But inviting the 'other woman' into her home and to her table, well that was downright remarkable... or crazy.

"I think those cards are pretty well mixed, Kathy," Bonnie said, knowing she'd keep shuffling incessantly if not reminded. "That was a wonderful thing to do, Val. And how did Susan seem to you? Did she appreciate the gesture?" Bonnie picked up her cards.

"Definitely, and Betsy was thrilled. She slept through 'til morning with no nightmares last night." Val looked at her cards and bid one club. The conversation continued between hands, and Val shared the changes she thought she was seeing in her foster child's mother.

The dealer just shook her head.

"What's going on, Kathy?" Bonnie asked. All her years as a clinical psychologist working with groups of students in her group processes classes, had allowed her to become quite adept at picking up on nonverbal cues from those around her.

"What? Oh, nothing really." Kathy looked at Val. "I just don't know how you do it. I mean from what I've heard about Susan lately, I wouldn't have her in my house."

Val smiled.

Bonnie also smiled with the wisdom of a woman who has witnessed much in life. "People really can change, Kathy, if they want it badly enough and have the love and support they need." Bonnie smiled then and looked over at Val. "But not everyone could do what you're doing, Val. You have an incredibly generous spirit."

Bonnie was amazed by the improvement she saw in her old friend Joe in such a short time. He seemed stronger every day. She sat by the side of his hospital bed listening to him complain about the food and picking on the nurses. Even without the little wink he put at the end of his complaint, she knew it was all in fun. Joe was one of the most easy-going men she'd ever known. She knew that was why Frank had always enjoyed their friendship. They both loved the Lord and their fellow man.

"I can't wait to break out of here," Joe was saying. "I'm going stir crazy, you know?"

"But how are you going to get along?" Bonnie was sure it would take quite some time for his leg to heal. He'd lived alone since his wife had passed away nearly five years ago.

"Oh, I've got that all figured out. Billy is going to get a nurse set up to come in every day, and he'll stop in a couple of times a week." Billy was Joe's youngest son. He and his wife lived right there in Madison, a few blocks from Joe. "Now I just need them to spring me from this joint," Joe chuckled, "but that's easier said than done. Enough about me. How are you doing?"

Bonnie recognized that his look of concern was full of love, not pity. He knew what it was like to lose a life partner. He knew the void it left—that unfillable void—and the effort it sometimes took to simply face a new day.

"I'm doing all right, Joe. I miss him every single day, of course, but Ginger has helped me not to feel so lonely. Oh here, I haven't shown you this one." She pulled up her latest picture of the little Teacup Pomeranian and held it out to him.

They chatted about the puppy, each of their families, and even the weather. When Bonnie looked at the time, she suggested she'd better be going.

She stood to leave but hesitated. "Joe, have they made any progress… I mean, are they any closer to finding who did this to you?"

"Oh, yeah. They found the car abandoned. One of the officers told me they were going to dust it for prints, but they won't really need them. I couldn't remember much of anything at first, but it's been coming back in bits and pieces. The important thing is, I saw the driver!"

CHAPTER FORTY-SIX

Susan stood in front of the brick building trying to push herself up the steps. She knew they had her wallet, but what else did they know? Screwing up her courage, she went in, identified herself, and explained she was there to pick up her wallet.

The officer behind the desk pulled out a manila envelope and slid her wallet out of it. He smiled, handed her a form, and said, "Just fill this out and sign at the bottom, and it's all yours. You're a lucky lady. It's not often we recover stolen property when somebody gets mugged."

Susan thanked him and quickly filled out the form. The officer handed the wallet to her, and she turned to leave, but when she reached the door, she turned back. "Excuse me…"

The officer who had already returned to another task, looked up. "Yes, ma'am?"

"Um, I was, uh, wondering… Officer Tomlin told me they found my wallet in a car, is that right?" He nodded. "Well, I was wondering if they knew who was driving the car."

"Not yet, but they're hoping to soon. They're dusting it for prints now."

Susan hoped her fake smile hid the fear suddenly crushing her chest.

Back outside, she hurried to the car where Nancy waited behind the wheel. Her entire body began to shake uncontrollably. She knew she had to get a grip on her nerves before Nancy got suspicious. *Breathe, Susan.* She took three controlled breaths, grateful for the sting of cold air… hoping it would subdue the burning flame she knew must be coloring her cheeks.

"Susan, what's wrong? Are you okay?"

Susan searched for an answer that would satisfy Nancy, but couldn't think clearly.

"What happened in there, hon? Talk to me."

Susan looked into the concerned eyes of her new sponsor, counselor, and friend and saw nothing but concern. "I… I don't know. I mean nothing really. I got my wallet back." She smiled weakly holding it up as evidence.

"But you're shaking. You look like you've seen a ghost or something."

"No, I mean, well, I guess maybe just having to go in there—well, you know—bad memories and all…"

Nancy reached over and gave her a hug. "You poor thing. I never thought about how that might make you feel. I should have gone in with you. But it's over now. Just sit back and relax. C'mon, let's get back to the house. Maybe a nice cup of calming tea when we get there, huh?"

"Thanks Nancy, that would be great." They rode the rest of the way in silence, but inside Susan was screaming.

♥

The early morning sun shone brightly through Susan's window giving the impression of warmth. Maybe it wouldn't be too cold for a walk to the hospital. *I need to see Uncle Joe. I have to tell him… before they do.*

Susan checked the weather forecast. The high was forecast to be forty-five degrees, no wind, mostly sunny. *Yes*, Susan thought, it was time to go to the hospital and face the music. She told Nancy where she was going—but not why—and Nancy offered to drive her. Susan still chose to walk. She might need time alone after talking to Joe… and she didn't know how much time she had left.

The policeman said they were dusting for fingerprints. Susan's stomach flipped just thinking about it. Her prints were on file, so it was only a matter of time. She hurried out the door and kept up a brisk pace the whole way to the hospital. Yet her steps slowed as she approached his room. She hesitated at the door then pushed herself through it.

Uncle Joe's bed was empty. The room was empty. There were no personal belongings… nothing.

Susan's heart stopped.

She rushed to the nurses' station. Thoughts raced through her head. *Did he have a setback? Did they miss something? Did he… No! He can't be dead!*

"Mr. Marconi… what happened to him? I mean, he's not in his room."

Seeing the dread on Susan's face, the young nurse quickly responded, "Oh no, it's all right. Are you a relative?"

"Yes! I'm Susan Walters. He's my uncle," Susan spoke with righteous indignation.

"Okay, well I'm sorry, ma'am, but Mr. Marconi was discharged this morning. A friend picked him up about twenty minutes ago." The nurse looked back down at the computer screen where she was entering patient data.

"Excuse me, but do you know who picked him up? Do you know where he went?"

"Why yes, actually. It was that nice Mrs. Dixon. Do you know her?"

Susan nodded.

"She's been in to visit with him every day and said she would drive him home so he didn't have to wait for his son to get off work."

Susan stood paralyzed.

"Are you okay, ma'am?"

"What? Oh, yes, thanks." Susan turned and walked down the hall with no idea where she was going.

Chapter Forty-Seven

"All right, Joe. What can I get for you?" Bonnie was amazed at how well her friend was managing on his crutches, but she could also see how it exhausted him.

"Now you've done enough, Bonnie. You saw me scooting along with my handy dandy crutches. I can manage."

"No, you can't. Not really. I can't exactly see you making yourself a sandwich and carrying that and maybe some chips and a drink while hanging onto your crutches." Bonnie laughed. "Sit down, you old fool."

Joe joined her and laughed at himself. He sat back on the big chaise his son had moved into the living room, and Bonnie helped him get his leg situated. The cast made it heavier than she had expected.

Joe Jr.'s wife had already stocked some groceries so Bonnie checked the refrigerator, found some ham and cheese, and made Joe a quick sandwich. "What would you like to drink? Can I fix you a cup of coffee or tea?"

"Did Lucy get any milk?"

"Let me check… yes," Bonnie called from the kitchen. "One big glass of milk coming up." She brought him the sandwich and milk along with a couple of the cookies she had baked the night before.

"A man could get used to service like this," Joe chuckled.

"Well don't get too used to it, but I'm happy to help out all I can. You certainly have done as much for me and Frank when we needed it. I do need to get home though and take care of Ginger. She loves her crate, but not for very extended periods of time. By now she's probably wondering where her momma is."

"Why don't you bring her with you when you come back? I'd love to meet her. I can tell from the pictures she's a real little charmer."

"Are you sure? You wouldn't mind if I bring her along?"

"No, not at all."

As Bonnie reached for her purse, her phone rang. She was surprised to see the name of an old friend on her caller ID. "Hmm, it's Susan Walters. Now why would she be calling me?"

"Well, you could answer it and find out." Joe winked, and Bonnie waved him off.

"I'm so sorry to bother you," Bonnie heard Susan speak quickly in her ear. "But they told me at the hospital you took Joe Marconi home this morning?" Bonnie confirmed, and Susan continued. "Well, I need to talk to my Uncle Joe… I know he's not really my uncle, I mean it's just by marriage, but that's how I think of him. Anyhow, I just really need to talk to him this morning if possible, but I don't have any way of getting there." She went on rapidly, "I'd take a taxi, but I'm short of funds right now, and—"

"Where are you?" Bonnie interrupted. "I'm heading home to get my little dog, and then I'll swing by and pick you up, okay?" She slipped her phone back into her purse, and tilted her head. "Well, that was kind of strange."

"What's up?" Now Joe's curiosity was piqued.

"That was Susan Walters. She wants to come and see you this morning but needs a ride. Oh my, I didn't even ask you whether you were all right to have her come visit."

"That's fine, and I'm not surprised." That piqued Bonnie's curiosity more, but Joe quickly added, "She came to see me in the hospital. I thought that was awfully thoughtful, but maybe she also misses having family. I think the girl is lonely."

Bonnie thought he suddenly looked quite sad himself and marveled at his compassion. "But the way she said it… well, there was a sense of urgency… but you're probably right. Maybe she's simply having a bad day and feeling lonely." Bonnie still wasn't so sure about that, but there was no sense upsetting or worrying Joe more. "Are you sure you're up for it? You look pretty tuckered out."

"No, I'm fine. I'll finish my sandwich and maybe take a little nap until you get back." He took another bite but looked like even that was an effort.

Bonnie smiled and decided she would take her time walking Ginger, picking up Susan, and getting back.

♥

Ginger was curled up in her little bed in the crate in the back of the car when Bonnie pulled up in front of the halfway house. As she pulled up, she saw the front door open immediately, and Susan dashed down the steps to climb in.

"Thank you for doing this, Bonnie. I really appreciate it," Susan said breathlessly.

"You're welcome. It was no problem really. Joe was kind of tired after the effort of getting ready to go home and then getting settled in, but he was going to rest while I ran home to get Ginger. He should be good by the time we get back over there."

"Ginger?" Susan asked looking up and down the street as though looking for someone.

Bonnie wondered what she was looking for. "Oh, that's right. You haven't met my little friend, Ginger. She's in the back." Bonnie smiled and Susan's head whipped around.

She looked back at Bonnie with a frown. Bonnie laughed to herself. *She thinks I've lost my mind or gone senile.* Then Bonnie laughed out loud. "Ginger is my little Teacup Pomeranian. She's in her crate all the way in the back."

"Oh, okay, I didn't know you had a dog. Didn't you used to have Molly years ago when I came to play cards at your house?"

"Yes, she was a good old girl, but we lost her over a year ago, and we didn't have it in us to get another dog when she died." Bonnie noticed Susan suddenly tense. "Are you okay, dear?"

"What? Oh... yes, yes, I'm fine. Just anxious to see Uncle Joe," Susan said. She had been looking out the back window but turned her attention back to Bonnie.

"Yes, you sounded really anxious when you called. Is it about anything in particular?" Bonnie wasn't one to pry, yet she couldn't help but wonder. This seemed like more than a simple visit to an uncle. What did she really want?

CHAPTER FORTY-EIGHT

Susan sat in the passenger side of Bonnie's car glancing nervously out the window. They were only blocks away when they passed a police car heading in the opposite direction. *Are they going to the halfway house? Do they know it was me? Oh God... wait, what did Bonnie say? Oh...*

Susan had lied. She said she was fine, but she wasn't fine at all. She had stood by the door of the halfway house waiting for Bonnie, terrified the police might show up first. That just couldn't happen. *Now what was Bonnie saying... something about the dog that died?* Then she remembered her *faux pas* the day Bonnie brought her home from the prison.

"Bonnie, I've been wanting to apologize to you."

"Why, what in the world for?"

"Well, the day I was released and you were so kind to pick me up, well, I'm so sorry. I hadn't heard about Frank." Susan saw Bonnie's expression change ever so slightly. The older woman quickly recovered her smile, but Susan saw the sadness sweep across Bonnie's face in that second.

Bonnie told her not to worry about it; it was okay. She understood Susan had no way of knowing. "Anyway, I sold the house, and Ginger and I now share a cottage at the Masonic Village. It's lovely, really."

Susan was trying to stay focused on what Bonnie was saying, but it was difficult not to scream. *If she would just drive a little faster...* She told herself to stop worrying. She hadn't told anyone where she was going. Well, actually she had told Nancy that a friend was picking her up to go visit her uncle who was just released from the hospital, but she hadn't told her where he lived.

Susan let out a sigh of relief when Bonnie finally pulled into Uncle Joe's driveway. Bonnie turned off the engine and started to get out.

"Oh, are you staying?" Susan thought she would just be dropping her off and leaving.

"I told Joe I'd bring Ginger to see him. Is that a problem?"

Susan saw a strange expression cross Bonnie's face. "No, no, of course not." Susan laughed weakly and headed for the door while Bonnie got Ginger out of her crate. "Oh, she's adorable!"

"Yes, I know. I love her to pieces. She's been the best medicine in the world for a lonely old woman."

"You're not an old woman," Susan said in all sincerity, "but I'm glad you have her." She had been about to knock when Bonnie pushed by her with a key for the front door.

"Joe gave me the key so he wouldn't have to struggle with his crutches when I come by. He's still getting used to them, and he's pretty weak right now."

Bonnie's words made Susan cringe. She had done this to him. One more thing she could never forgive herself for doing.

The front door of Joe's ranch-style house opened right into the great-room where Joe was lying on the chaise in the living room area. Both women saw from the way he raised his head, he had been sleeping, but his face lit up at the sight of them.

"Come in, ladies! It's so good to see you, Susan."

Susan wondered if he would still think so when she was finished what she had come for.

"Oh, and there are three ladies who have come to visit me. Bring that little one over here, Bonnie."

Bonnie handed Ginger over to him, and the pup immediately planted kisses all over his face. He didn't seem to mind at all and laughed at her friendly greeting. Bonnie took the dog back after a couple of minutes, worried she would exhaust him.

"So how are you doing, Susan?" Joe asked smiling in her direction.

Susan thought she saw something more behind his smile. *Does he already know? No... how could he?* "That's what I should be asking you, Uncle Joe," she said trying to cover her anxiety. "I'm okay... for now... but that's what I want to talk to you about," she added.

"Why don't I take Ginger out for a little walk and give you some privacy?" Bonnie offered.

"No, really Bonnie, you don't have to do that. I think you should hear this."

Susan saw the look of curiosity match Uncle Joe's. *They're both going to hate me.* Susan took the seat closest to Joe, folded her hands in her lap, and searched for the words.

"What is it, Sue?" Joe leaned forward and the crease between his brows deepened... he looked truly concerned about her... loving in spite of what she'd done to his nephew, Marty.

Susan nearly changed her mind—though she realized she had no choice—because she dreaded the change she knew her confession would bring about. She breathed in deeply and charged ahead. "Uncle Joe, you know about my drinking problem... no, let me call it like it is, I'm an alcoholic."

Joe nodded. He wore a knowing smile that also said, 'yes, and it's okay.'

Susan forced herself to continue. "Well I've been sober for the last few weeks, ever since... well, ever since something happened, and I realized I was out of control."

Joe tried to interrupt. She thought he probably wanted to say he was glad, but she had to keep going.

She felt the burning in her face and neck but pushed on. "The thing that happened, the thing that made me realize I had to stop... it was the night of your accident. It was the night someone hit you with their car and then drove away." Susan couldn't control the quiver in her voice, and she felt the hot tears rolling down her cheeks.

Joe looked totally confused.

"Uncle Joe, it was me." Her voice cracked.

"What was you?" he asked. "What are you talking about?" His face was lined with incredulity.

"It was *me,*" Susan said more emphatically. "I was driving that car." Susan looked over and saw the look of shock and disbelief on Bonnie's face. But Joe Marconi looked even more confused. *He doesn't understand. Oh God... help me.*

"No, Susan. I don't know what you're talking about, but it wasn't you. You were not driving the car that hit me."

Susan insisted it was.

"What makes you think it was you?" he asked. "I mean how can you possibly think that?"

"I was drunk, Uncle Joe. I'm so sorry." She gasped for air… couldn't stop the tears. "I had rented the car with a false ID, and… and then I bought this bottle of vodka. I was upset. I missed Elizabeth, and I thought I just had to have a drink," she sobbed. "Then I just kept drinking, and then well, I don't remember everything, but I woke up in the park. I had a terrible gash on my forehead. I guess I bumped my head… must have slammed on the brakes… but I didn't know. I swear, I didn't know… I, I heard about the hit-and-run on the news, and… and then I heard it was you… and—"

Bonnie was handing her tissues and put an arm around her. *Why is she trying to comfort me? Don't they understand?*

Uncle Joe was leaning forward trying to reach her. Saying her name. But she had to keep going. "Uncle Joe, the police found the car, and they found my wallet inside it. They thought I'd been mugged and the person who mugged me was driving the car that hit you."

She took a breath to try to control her sobs and finish the telling.

"They said they were dusting the car for prints and were hoping to catch the driver, but they're going to find my prints. Uncle Joe, I had to tell you before they come to arrest me. I had to tell you I didn't know. I never would have left you. I swear I wouldn't."

"Susan, listen to me!" Joe raised his voice to be heard above her sobs. "It wasn't you! I know it wasn't you. I *saw* the driver before he hit me. It happened fast, but I saw the car coming at me. I couldn't move… Couldn't get back on the curb, but I saw the driver clearly. *It was a man, Susan!* It *wasn't* you!"

Susan saw Joe and Bonnie exchange knowing glances. Susan couldn't understand why he was saying that.

"Susan, listen to me. What do you remember? I mean exactly what do you remember from that night?" he asked.

Susan explained she must have blacked out because she couldn't remember anything between drinking in the park and waking up in the bushes. She didn't even know how she'd gotten there.

It wasn't easy for Joe to convince her he was telling the truth. She thought he was somehow trying to save her. She knew it was no use. Her fingerprints would be in the car.

But then Bonnie said something that changed everything. "Susan, Joe told me the other day that he had seen the man who hit him. He was even able to give the police a description of the guy's face."

Stunned, Susan fell back into the nearby chair. *I didn't do it?* Was it possible she wouldn't have to go back to prison? Could she really have a second chance to make things right and get her daughter back?

It took a while, but as Susan talked it out with Uncle Joe and Bonnie, she started to put the pieces of the puzzle together. Some were still missing, but she remembered sitting on the bench in the park. She remembered looking around feeling hopeless. Then she remembered…

"Oh my God," Susan's eyes widened, "The man on the bridge!"

CHAPTER FORTY-NINE

Bonnie couldn't believe all that had happened in the past couple of days. She headed to Val's early for the weekly bridge game.

Val met her at the door, took her coat, and told her to go on into the family room where Andy was waiting. When Val came back, Bonnie told them a lot had changed in Susan's life.

"Well, you know, Andy and I both thought she seemed different when she was here for dinner," Val interjected. "She seemed, I don't know, maybe calmer."

Andy agreed.

"That's because she's sober," Bonnie said. "I don't mean like between binges. I mean she has finally acknowledged she has a problem, and she's doing something about it."

Listening, Val smiled and took her husband's hand.

"She actually said the words, 'I'm an alcoholic' when she was talking to Joe this afternoon. But there's so much more." Bonnie recounted the events of the day, including Susan's admission of what she thought she had done and her shock at learning she was not to blame. "Once she'd recovered and had time to absorb it all, Susan told me something that nearly broke my heart. She had actually planned to ask me to bring her here so she could see Elizabeth one more time before the police came to get her. Can you imagine?"

Andy shook his head. "My God, she must have been going through hell." He turned and looked at his wife. "I know she did this to herself, but I can't help feeling sorry for her."

Val nodded her agreement.

"Yes," Bonnie said, "you should have seen her. It was heart-breaking to watch. I know she's messed up… a lot… but I think for her, this was hitting bottom. She thought she had lost her child forever. I'm convinced she wants to change."

"I think you might be right," Val said touching her husband's shoulder. "I hope so, for Betsy's sake."

"And speaking of Betsy," Andy stood as he spoke, "I'd better see if her movie is almost over. She's been watching *Beauty and the Beast*... again," he laughed. "But I checked the time on it and I'm guessing it's real close to the end."

Bonnie helped Val put out the refreshments, and the doorbell rang just as Andy and Betsy headed for the garage. Betsy skipped out the door, always excited to go spend time with Mia and the rest of the youngest Reeds. She still had no idea she was actually their aunt.

♥

Val greeted her guests at the door with a comfortable smile. She felt lighter than she had for some time. "Kathy, you changed your hair. I love it!"

"Thanks, Sarah did it for me."

Sarah had been a hairdresser studying psychology when she'd first joined the bridge group, but she obviously hadn't lost her talent for coloring and styling.

Kathy's face was framed with a luscious, warm chestnut shag that softened her. "I finally decided I'm over the blonde," she laughed.

Sarah, who had followed her in, added, "Yep, I think this really suits her. Looks good, right?"

Bonnie and Val both agreed emphatically.

"She fought me tooth and nail, but I finally wore her down."

Kathy laughed. "She did, and now I love it... and so does hubby," she winked. "I look so hot!"

Everyone got a kick out of Kathy's remarks, and Val was grateful for the lighter topic. She'd had enough of the heavy talk she and Bonnie had been sharing about another, former blonde member of their bridge club.

"Did Betsy and Grandpa leave yet?" Sarah asked.

"They just headed to the car. I might be able to catch them..." Val turned toward the kitchen as she said it.

"No, no, you don't need to. I was just going to tell Betsy something, but she'll find out when she gets to the house."

Val's eyebrows shot up. "Why, what's going on?"

Sarah had everyone's attention now. Her face broke out into a big grin. "We got the kids a puppy!"

Jaws dropped and Kathy was the first to respond. "Oh my gosh! Are you crazy? I mean getting a puppy when you've got a baby on the way? Holy crap!"

"That's exactly why we decided to get it now. Once the baby comes, we're going to be too busy changing diapers to have time for housebreaking a puppy. And the kids have been begging us to get a dog. Actually, I think Craig wanted it most of all, and he promised he and the kids will take care of her." Sarah grabbed her phone and showed them all a couple of pictures. "The kids voted on the name—and I know it's not very original for a golden retriever—but meet Goldie."

That's when Bonnie chimed in with, "Well I can't wait to start having play dates with Ginger and Goldie… and I can't wait to beat you and Kathy this week. Let's play!"

The ladies gathered around the table, and Val was delighted when she and Bonnie made their first contract… and their second. It was their night for sure. She had no trouble following the bidding or taking tricks. Her partner smiled knowingly, and Val knew she understood. Bonnie never did miss much.

♥

Val was so tickled, she was still crowing about it hours later when she and Andy got ready for bed. "You know it is a bit more fun when you win, and we certainly put those young'uns back in their place tonight."

Andy laughed at his wife's good-humored bragging. She knew he was happy for her, but from the expression on his face, she suspected he'd heard enough. She saw something else written in his eyes.

He came up behind her and drew her into his embrace. "All right, wifey," he murmured, "enough about the ladies and your bridge game."

He pulled her down onto the bed and teased, "It's time for a different kind of game, don't you think?"

Andy ran his fingers through her hair and gently drew her closer until their lips met. The warmth that ran through Val's body at her husband's touch melted away all thoughts of bridge, all thoughts of Susan and Betsy, all thoughts of anything but the desire he'd awakened.

EPILOGUE

"Come on, Bobby!"

Andy could hear the exasperation in Elizabeth's voice.

"Hurry up! Oh. My. Goodness. He's so slow."

Mia laughed, "He's coming, sweetie. Come sit by me, Betsy."

Elizabeth had gotten used to having different names. Her mother and teachers still called her Elizabeth. All the Reeds called her Betsy, and to her daddy, she would forever be Lizzy. And to her it was just as it should be. She hopped up onto the big sectional between Mia and Julie, and the three girls cuddled under Mia's big furry blanket. Goldie wagged her tail then settled at Julie's feet where she could almost always be found.

Andy sat across the room and observed it all with contented amusement. He knew Betsy didn't mind that her mother had a meeting tonight because she got to have a sleepover with Mia and Julie.

"So which movie did you guys decide on?" Craig asked. "And where's your brother?"

"We're watching *Frozen*," Mia said. "Betsy picked it."

"Yeah," Cody groaned, "we've only seen it like a hundred times. That's why Bobby *isn't* coming. He said he can't stand to watch it one more time."

It amazed Andy how the older children humored Betsy. Especially the girls. And, as much as he hated secrets, he wondered if they could ever explain to his grandchildren that this little girl was their aunt... their father's sister. But he had reconciled that—at least for now—that was best left a family secret.

"Well, do you want to go in the other room and we can watch something else?" Craig asked Cody. "I bet we can find something on ESPN."

"Yeah Dad, cool!" Cody bounded off his end of the couch and headed toward the bedrooms. "I'll go get Bobby."

"What's wrong, Betsy?" Craig asked.

Her lower lip protruded and her chin started to quiver. "Aren't you going to do movie night with us?" she whined.

"Not this time. I'm going to go hang out with the boys, but Aunt Sarah will be in as soon as she gets Destiny settled, and Grandpa Andy will do movie night with you." Craig winked at his Dad and made his escape.

"Oh yeah," Betsy laughed, "I forgot about Grandpa Andy."

"You forgot me? I'm hurt!" Andy feigned his crushing disappointment, and Mia and Julie joined Betsy's giggles.

"What's going on in here?" Sarah asked returning without the baby in her arms. "Sounds like a party… even though it looks like the guys have deserted us."

"Hey!"

"Oops, sorry Grandpa," Sarah laughed.

"Is the baby asleep? Can we start it now?" Betsy was at the end of her patience.

Sarah nodded and plopped down next to Julie. "Yes, Destiny is finally settled. Go ahead, sweetie. Push play."

Andy looked at his daughter-in-law with admiration. She had to be exhausted, but she never showed it. She'd been doing an amazing job of raising four children, and now, with the new baby, she still seemed to balance it all—with the help of Craig, of course—and never complained. *My son is a lucky man.*

♥

Susan nervously walked to the front of the hall. "Hi, my name is Susan, and I'm an alcoholic."

"Hi, Susan," came the response from several dozen people gathered there.

Susan took a deep breath. "It has been one year since my last drink… and I appreciate the special guests who have come here tonight to help me celebrate." Her vision blurred with tears as she looked out at Uncle Joe, Bonnie, and Val. She could hardly believe how blessed she was. "I nearly destroyed my life, and I hurt the people I loved most before I hit my personal bottom."

Susan caught movement in the back of the room. Someone just arriving. She gasped.

He came!

Marty smiled at her and took the empty seat by his Uncle Joe. She had invited him, but she didn't think he'd actually come. Once Susan had regained custody of her daughter and she and Elizabeth were settled into a regular routine, she had contacted Marty and invited him back into their lives. He'd been hesitant at first, but his love for the child he still thought of as his own, must have motivated him to give it a try.

Elizabeth spent every other weekend with her 'Daddy' now and often had playdates with her older nieces and nephews. Susan thanked God every day for their expanded family and for the acceptance and forgiveness they'd given.

Regaining her composure, she smiled and continued to share a brief version of her story. It was tough, but she knew it was part of the process, part of what worked for her. She didn't blame her mother anymore, although she understood how her childhood had contributed to her addictive personality. But now she accepted responsibility for her own choices. She acknowledged that she was powerless over her addiction, and she had surrendered to her higher power… Susan had turned back to God.

♥

"Andy, you should have heard her. It's hard to believe she's the same woman who was such a wreck just a year ago." Val dropped onto the bed exhausted, but so wound up the words kept tumbling out. "And after the meeting, when everyone was mingling and having refreshments, I saw her talking with Marty. They really seemed to be getting along."

"I know they've been amicable for months, and that's been good for Betsy. She has her daddy back in her life and I'm just Grandpa Andy."

Those words were music to Val's ears. She had missed little Betsy when the girl was first reunited with her mother, but fortunately they still got to see her often. And Val had her life back.

"But there's more," Val went on. "She came over to spend time with us after that, and Marty was just kind of standing to the side munching on a cookie. So, Bonnie asked Susan to let her know when she was ready to go—since she and Joe were her ride—but then Susan said thanks, *but*…" Val paused, turned to face her husband, and spoke slowly with a wistful smile, "…she and Marty were going to go for coffee *and* he was going to take her home."

Andy's eyes widened. "Really? Do you think—"

"That maybe they'll get back together?" Val jumped in. "Well, I don't know, but wouldn't that be great for Betsy?" *Wouldn't it be great for everyone!* She flopped back against the pillows and began to relax. "So, when I left, Bonnie and Joe walked me to the car. I'm so glad the two of them have started spending more time together. I mean, I don't think they're serious or anything, but they're so cute as a couple."

"Cute?" Andy chuckled moving closer to take his wife in his arms.

Val poked him with her elbow. "You know what I mean."

"Yes ma'am, I know what you mean. And I think *you're* cute," Andy said sitting up leaning on one elbow.

With his other hand he stroked her hair and slowly slid his hand down her cheek.

"No, I take it back. I think you're beautiful."

Val warmed at his touch and was amazed that he could still have that effect on her. When his lips met hers, she forgot about Susan and Marty. She forgot about Bonnie and Joe. She forgot everything but the man in her arms.

ABOUT THE AUTHOR

Gloria Bostic is a retired special education teacher from York, Pennsylvania. As a Masters level clinical psychologist, she also worked with women and children to help them overcome abuse. She lives in Dover, PA, with her husband, Lee, and enjoys spending time with her three sons and grandchildren.

Also by Gloria Bostic...

Greta Friedman travels from victim to victory in this story of a young woman's search for the life she's been denied. A childhood filled with loss and abuse leaves her desperate to find love and normalcy, but as a young adult Greta is frustrated by unanswered prayers and a pattern of relationships that end badly... until she meets someone special. When Gabe Engel mysteriously comes into her life, Greta begins the journey that will give her the strength to escape impending danger and finally make her dreams a reality.

Valerie Reed is plagued by migraines, insomnia, and a growing anxiety that her happily-ever-after is about to come crumbling down. Tormented by the fear of losing her husband of nearly thirty years, she hangs onto the one thing she knows she can count on—her friendship with the women in her bridge group. They provide a safe-haven with warmth, laughter, and trust... until that trust is broken. As Val searches for a way to save her marriage and learn to trust again, her life and her bridge group go through unanticipated transformations. Their lives will never be the same, and Val wonders if the power of prayer will be enough to save them all.

The Greatest Aunt

Gloria Bostic
Illustrated by Vicki Friedman

It's a scary time for Flora when she learns her parents must go away. She will have to go live with her great-aunt, but can't understand why they call her great. Flora happily discovers why and agrees!

www.ingramcontent.com/pod-product-compliance
Lightning Source LLC
Chambersburg PA
CBHW060922180626
46817CB00004B/1361